Copyright © Ni[...]

All rights reserved, including th[...]
book, or portions of this book thereof, in any form. No part of this text may be reproduced, transmitted, downloaded, decompiled, reverse engineered, or stored in or introduced to any information storage and retrieval system, in any form or by any means, whether electronic or mechanical without the express written permission of the author. The scanning, uploading, and distribution of this book via the internet or via any other means without the permission of the author is illegal and punishable by law. Please purchase only authorised electronic editions and do not participate in, or encourage, electronic piracy of these copyrighted materials.

As always for my children, for you are the stories that I am still helping to write.

About the author

Born in 1970 in Pembrokeshire, West Wales, Nigel Shinner is a fledgling thriller author. Although, writing for pleasure since the mid 1990s, Nigel only self-published his first book, FROM WITHIN in 2015. With a small but loyal reader base, Nigel hopes to expand on this with his new novel THE LEGACY and the sequel to FROM WITHIN under the title of THE MINDSWEEPER.

Nigel currently works for a local charity and lives with his partner and youngest child in his home town of Milford Haven. He also has two older children from a previous relationship.

Nigel Shinner is currently in the employment of The Paul Sartori Foundation (reg. charity no. 513079)

The Paul Sartori Foundation is a registered charity offering Hospice at Home Care to people of Pembrokeshire living in the later stages of any life-limiting illness. The Foundation also aims to help and support those close to the patient during the illness and throughout the bereavement period.

The author would like to donate ten percent of the royalty of this title toward The Paul Sartori Foundation and thus further support Pembrokeshire's only hospice at home service.

If any readers would like to donate to such a worthy cause then please visit:-

care.paulsartori.org

THE LEGACY

BY

NIGEL SHINNER

Chapter One

The groaning had stopped. There was very little movement. The figure blind folded and tied to the chair had given up the fight. In a dark dank abandoned warehouse in the middle of nowhere, illuminated only by car headlights, was where this poor soul would meet his end.

Robert Jones stood staring at the man he had abducted nearly twenty-four hours ago. In a strange way he admired the man. When Jones was asked to do a job like this, the subjects were never usually this strong or resilient. He was used to grown men crying like babies and wetting themselves through fear. What he called interrogation was actually torture. But torture was more effective than questions alone.

Jones wore two sets of decorator's paper coveralls over his naked, hairless body and plastic shoe covers over a pair of cheap generic trainers. He had his body waxed regularly so he would have no hair to shed. No hair shed would mean there were no follicles for DNA identification. Nothing was left to chance. He did not smoke, so there were no cigarettes butts with his saliva on. No identifying tattoos, scars or features. He very rarely spoke except to ask direct questions. And those he did speak to would never reveal who he was as his voice was the last they heard.

The man in the chair lifted his head. The silence in the room had opened up the possibility that maybe he was alone and the punishment had ceased for good. Perhaps he would survive. Sure, he would be psychologically scarred for life but he would live. That was what was important.

What he did not hear was the silencer being slowly screwed onto the end of the handgun.

The restrained man flinched in his seat as he heard the soft padding footsteps behind him. He twisted and turned but he could not see Jones in the dimly lit shadows away from the headlights.

There was no more flinching once the bullet had passed through his skull. The debris from the exit wound sprayed across the plastic sheeting spread around the chair. The bullet was designed to expand and fragment on impact so not to leave any ballistics evidence. This is how professionals work.

Robert Jones was a professional but Robert Jones was not his real name. He had not answered to his real name for a decade or more. Robert could be Rob, Bob or Rab depending on where he was working and Jones could be James, John or Johnson. One day he was Bob Johnson, the next he was Robert John. The vagueness of the name made his anonymity easier.

There were no bulletin boards or Yellow Pages for professional hitmen. Although, he did not think of himself as a hitman. He would do the dirty work that was too dirty for the more organised criminal collectives. Abduction, interrogation, investigation, the acquiring of items and murder; the skill set required for such work was wide and varied.

This particular job was one that he fitted in whilst working another. The instruction was simple, 'get as much information about an incoming shipment as possible'. The poor lifeless body before him had belonged to a dock security guard who was employed to turn a blind eye when particular boats came into the harbour. Jones never asked the questions first, he would always 'soften up' the subject beforehand. He found this method worked best.

The softening up of this individual comprised of pounding his lower limbs with a steel pipe. This served two purposes; kept the subject alive as there were no organs to rupture, and it prevented the subject from escaping easily as bones would often be broken. Once the information was acquired, then the subject could be disposed of.

The other job he was halfway through was a significantly more challenging task altogether. The brief had been to locate and acquire a particular item; an antique shotgun, and eliminate anyone looking for the item but make it look like an accident if possible. The job came with a six figure paycheque, so was well worth the effort.

Just forty-eight hours earlier he had helped a man to his death from the top of a five storey building site. An easy accident to construct, he just needed to create the opportunity. The shotgun eluded him this time and finding the item would be more difficult than he first thought, but he did have some resources at his disposal.

The only thing that he did not calculate was that there would be others looking for the item. They would be just as determined, just as ruthless but nowhere near as professional. And that made them dangerous.

Chapter Two

David Hill sat on his kitchen counter and stared at the floor. He did not want to believe the news but he had no choice. If life had not been cruel enough to him over the last few years, then this was life dealing him the final bad hand of a game he was never meant to win. His father was dead.

Unlike most bereaved sons, David could not look back at the cherished moments of his childhood where his father had been a factor, because for the most part, he had not been there at all. An estrangement that had only recently been overcome; the father/son relationship had just started to flourish thirty odd years too late, and now it would never be realised.

David's parents had had a turbulent relationship while they were together. Pam, David's mother was only sixteen when he was born. She felt her life had been robbed by the child she did not want but hoped it would keep the man she loved. But as with so many young men, a child would not make him stay. John Hill was a young hard working brickie who wanted to work hard and play even harder. A clingy girlfriend with a screaming child would just inhibit his life. He left and moved away.

Pam realised that she would not find a new man with a child in tow and promptly left the infant with her parents to seek the life she wanted, a life that would involve alcohol, weed and men; all in large quantities.

David grew up very quickly. His grandparents did the best they could but they were in their late fifties when their youngest daughter decided to disappear. By the time David hit his twenty-first birthday both his grandparents had passed away. In that time he had only seen his mother about a dozen times and most of those when he was too young to remember the events well.

Needless to say, David Hill had become a very independent young man. He worked hard and paid his way through various college courses. Being a qualified electrical engineer had proved to be lucrative and he had made a decent life for himself. His last engineering job had brought him to the West Wales town of Milford Haven. It had been the best eight years of his life. He had formed bonds and made some good friends. For the first time in his life he had felt like he belonged somewhere.

The last he had heard anything of his mother was when a half-sister, who he never knew he had, contacted him to say that their mother had died of cancer. Even though he did travel to the funeral, there were no feelings of loss for him. The maternal bond had never been there. He did meet his half-sister and two half-brothers but the family connection was fragile at best and after a few months, all communication was lost. Although, during that time, all he learned about his mother was that she had been as equally a bad mother to his siblings as she had been to him. Four children from three different men and not a suitable father figure among them. His mother's funeral was five years ago and not once did he look back or feel any sorrow.

An existence without a connection to any blood relatives looked like a certainty until three years ago.

While browsing his social media, David received a message via Facebook asking if he was a David Hill that had grown up in the Bristol area. Also, if his mother was called Pam and his father was John Hill. The message came directly from a John Hill.

When David saw the profile picture he could see instantly the family resemblance. He had the same features as his father, large deep green eyes, wide smile and sharp angled jawline. His complexion was the same, as was his hairline as he settled into his thirties. There were no issues of abandonment; he just wanted to have a relationship with a real family member.

A reply message turned into a phone call. A phone call turned into a meeting. After a few more meetings and phone calls, spaced across a year or so, David returned to Bristol to stay over with his father and his father's girlfriend, Rachel. There were no other brothers and sisters waiting for him, just a successful construction company owner and a girlfriend younger than the estranged son that was coming to visit. David felt the inner comfort that only family intimacy brings. He now knew what happy felt like.

He shared two Christmases and a family holiday abroad. Even when he lost his job, because of the collapse of a company buy out, it did not keep David down for long.

His good friend, Tom McDonald, had secured a job as a security guard for the now closed refinery and managed to find a few shifts for David. It meant less money and he had to downsize his house for a flat, but it did not matter as David had found the missing element in his life. More money or less money, it was of no concern, he was content.

That was until today. He was numb from the news. A very tearful Rachel had called to tell David that his father was dead. He felt sorry for her having to phone him and say that her boyfriend had passed away. It was his father that had died yet he felt sorry for her. But that was how he was, unselfish.

He promised to travel up as soon as he could to help with the arrangements or to support in any way he could.

After the call ended, he rang Tom to tell him the bad news. Tom was the only person he told everything to, regardless of what it was. They were the best of friends. If this is what having a brother felt like, then David was grateful for it. Tom said that he would come straight over.

David stayed sitting on the kitchen counter top after he hung up. He would not move until he had a reason too. Life had dealt him a cruel blow and everything could wait for him.

Chapter Three

It was a cloudy, moonless night. The vast country garden was shrouded in darkness. The sizeable house cut out the light from any surrounding sources to add to the inky blackness the night had already provided. The house could also be empty. With no lights inside or cars parked outside to indicate presence, the job would be considerably improved task. Tonight was as good a chance as they would get.

"Stay here and keep your eyes open!" Jimmy said to his brother in hushed tones through his balaclava.

Billy stayed silent and nodded. Billy always did as he was told. Jimmy knew best. As the older brother, he was also the boss. A quick smash and grab was what they were hoping for but things never turned out the way they were planned.

Jimmy edged towards the back door of the house. There was no PIR activated light like so many houses have, so the furtive approach could continue without alerting the neighbours or even the occupants, if there were any.

He pressed his back against the cold red brick wall next to the back door and shone a small LED light through the glass. There were no signs of life. He could just make out the end of a key which was in the lock. The door was an old wooden type with several glass panels in the top half. Jimmy knew that he could open the door cleanly with just a kick.

Jimmy looked towards his brother and gave him a thumb's up. In the dim light he could see Billy raise his hand and repeat the signal. The coast was clear.

With a single firm kick to the lock, the door swung open with a crash. In a second, Jimmy was through the door and making his way deeper into the substantial house. Billy quickly followed his brother carrying a small bright flashlight to illuminate the task in hand.

Jimmy ducked into a room at the far end of the central corridor of the house. The shadows caused by his brother's light danced against the wall and the cabinet that was the focus of the robbery.

"Hold the fucking light still!" Said Jimmy in an angry muted voice.

"Sorry Jimmy." The reply was at a normal volume and not showing the caution of someone trying to go unheard.

The retort came with an open palm to the side of the head.

"Shut it!" The voice was still muted but the increased anger in the statement raised the tone by a few decibels. There was no reply this time.

The brothers stood in silence for a moment, just in case there was somebody to wake in the house. They heard nothing. Jimmy turned his attention back onto the cabinet and pointed a finger toward it as an instruction of where the light should be pointed.

Once the light focussed onto the antique glass panelled doors, Jimmy placed a crow bar into the gap. With one swift action, the doors flung open exposing the contents. Twelve valuable, antique shotguns stood like soldiers within their individual wooden apertures.

Jimmy started to load up the large sack his brother now held open, dropping the weapons in two at a time. Once the cabinet was empty, Jimmy cast his own LED light over the rest of the room to check for any other valuables. They had come solely for the guns but if an opportunity for a quick score presented itself to the brothers then they would take it. A swift scan revealed no obvious pickings or at least, nothing worth the risk.

Jimmy led the way back into the corridor. But before he could check to see if his brother was following him, something struck him on the side of the head.

"Get out! You bastards!" said the voice in the dark.

Jimmy turned the LED towards a short, portly old man in pyjamas brandishing a walking stick. The light took the man more by surprise than the blow to the head did to Jimmy and the old man raised his hand across his eyes.

"Fuck Off!" Jimmy screamed in the direction of the old man. They were found out so volume was no longer a problem.

He swung the crowbar but the old man managed to parry the blow with his walking stick. This was not repeated as Jimmy swung another rapid stroke toward his elderly attacker. The man fell to the ground.

"Get to the van. Start the engine, and keep your eyes open." The elder brother said to his sibling. Billy made his way through the house and to the van.

Jimmy turned to the stricken man before him.

"YOU...DIDN'T...SEE...FUCK...ALL! OK?" Each word was punctuated with a kick to the figure whimpering in the darkness. The strike with the crowbar had been enough to incapacitate the man but Jimmy cared little for anybody's welfare when he was on a score.

Jimmy stood for a moment over the now seriously injured man. He shone the light. Blood dripped from a head wound and the nose of the person he assumed was the elderly home owner. Violence was just a small part of what Jimmy considered was necessary. He kicked the fallen man one last time and then fled into the night.

Chapter Four

David was still sat on the kitchen counter, nursing a lukewarm mug of coffee when Tom let himself into the flat.

> "Hey buddy." Tom's greeting was cautious.
>
> "Thanks for coming man." David sounded defeated.
>
> "No problem."

There was an awkward silence between the friends for a moment. Neither could look at each other. There was nothing to be said that would help change what had happened. No words of wisdom. No profound statements to ease the atmosphere.

After a suitable pause, Tom decided he would take charge of the situation, like he did most of the time. But then that was Tom.

> "So, do you want a big man hug then?" Tom stood

with his arms spread ready to embrace his friend.

David said nothing. He hopped off the counter, smiled at his pal and accepted the hug. They stood together patting each other on the back and squeezing like only good friends can.

> "Right, let me go, you freak! People will talk and not

about how good looking I am." Tom winked at his friend as he released him. No matter the circumstances, Tom would always find something funny to say. His philosophy was that every problem should be faced with a sense of humour.

"You're such a twat!" David laughed.

"I'm your twat, brethren."

David made fresh coffee and sat with his comrade. They talked about the usual things that cemented their friendship. Films, music and going to the pub. There were never any quiet moments between the two men. Even if David wanted some silence, Tom would forbid such nonsense and just continue to talk, but then he would make up stories and tell jokes to force the conversation to start again.

A true friend was hard to come by but that is exactly what David had found in Tom. Coincidence had brought them together and their desire to pursue a friendship had kept them together.

The two had started to work on one of the local refineries on the same day, but because of the close knit community of the locals, some of the outsiders were made to feel just like that; outsiders. Tom was a local boy and did not see things the same way as his home-grown colleagues.

At lunch on their first day in the new job, Tom noticed David sitting on his own, staring into his food and playing with it. He was not alone for long. Tom simply walked up to the table and sat opposite him, uninvited.

"If you sit there much longer emanating all that charisma you're gonna be drawing a crowd, so I thought I'd pop over and save you from yourself." The opening address from Tom was delivered with wink of his right eye, which was how he indicated he was being sarcastic to the lesser informed. David laughed and held out his hand, they introduced each other and had been friends ever since.

David did not know it yet but he would come to rely on Tom more over these next few days than he ever had before and owe him more than he could ever repay.

Chapter Five

Jones was not angry but disappointed. He had heard about the robbery at The Old Manse and was surprised that someone had got there before him. The online news report also said that the owner, Captain Warden, had been beaten to the point of death but had survived. Jones almost laughed out loud even though laughter was not something that he participated in often, unless it was necessary to have a psychotic laugh at someone else's expense. He wondered which local journalist had used to the line 'beaten to the point of death but had survived'. If he had beaten somebody to the point of death, then death would have been a certainty.

The disappointment he felt was not only for the fact that someone had beaten him to his next target but that someone else was looking for the same item, the antique shotgun. Also this someone, although an amateur, was motivated, able and vicious. He cursed the report, for while it had over dramatized the events of the previous evening, it had not given any details on the offender or offenders, but then that was usual when the crime was only a few hours old. There were no descriptions or numbers given. A solo burglar might be an opportunist or someone like him, under contract. But a gang would possibly be part of a larger organisation. That was his experience and he was rarely wrong.

He clicked off the story and drank what was left of the coffee he had made about an hour earlier. Coffee always accompanied the fruit that was his breakfast every morning.

The bed was already pushed to one side as the hotel room was not as spacious as he would have liked. Budget hotels were always hit or miss. He needed the room to exercise. The workout was a rigid interval training program to maintain his physical endurance, followed by a martial arts drill to keep him well practiced with moves he did not need to use unless absolutely necessary, but also keeping his reflexes and reaction time at an optimum.

Once the morning routine had finished, he would need to start the search again and hit the road. One night was all he ever stayed in hotels like this. He paid cash and always used false identification. Not that anyone could tell the difference as his passport and driver's license were expensive and indistinguishable from the real thing. He even had a false bank account with the appropriate cards and fake statements so he could hire cars as and when he needed them or if a hotel needed a swipe of a debit card. These were all tools of his trade.

His other tools were in a bag tucked under the bed. These were the ones that if he showed them to you then it was unlikely that the outcome was going to be favourable. In the bag was a telescopic baton, as used by the police, a push button tactical lock knife, which was rarely used, and the most important items of his tool bag; two Glock 17 handguns, one with a threaded muzzle to fit a silencer. Also in the bag were two spare magazine clips and two boxes of ammo; one of hollow points and one with full metal jackets. The hollow points were designed to expand in flight thus causing maximum damage to the target, usually used for a one shot kill. The FMJs were designed to cause the least amount damage to a target, often used by hunters not wishing to spoil a trophy pelt. Although, all bullets were designed to kill, in the hands of a profession, a firearm could be used more precisely, almost surgically. Wounding was frequently required.

With the morning routine finished, he showered and dressed. Just as much effort was put into the anonymity of his clothing as it was for himself. All his clothes fit well as not to draw attention by being too big or too small. Also, all the labels were removed to prevent identification of an outlet of purchase. The clothes were typically basics with no logos or distinguishing features. Plain shirts or t-shirts, plain trousers, jeans or cargo pants, or if the job required a cheap but modern style suit, again with all identifying labels removed; the wardrobe of this kind of professional was not filled with Armani or other such designer labels, as the movies would have you believe.

The final task was to wipe the room for prints and pour bleach down the sink and into the shower. This was to contaminate or destroy any possible DNA trace. Obsession and paranoia is what kept him at the top of his game.

Chapter Six

After a couple of hours chatting and emptying the fridge of all but one can of beer. Tom left David to it. It was still early evening and the two friends would usually be together until it was very late. Either chatting, watching a movie or playing on a console; all would be accompanied with a four pack or two of whatever was on offer that week in the supermarket booze aisle.

But tonight was different. David was different. He was hurting more than he would admit to his friend. Tom sensed it and left.

Rachel phoned to confirm the funeral arrangements and they discussed accommodation. David was happy to stay at a hotel but Rachel wanted him to stay at the house with her. The agreement also involved Tom coming along for support. The house was big enough, so it was not a problem.

David could not help but feel that there was something wrong. Although it was right that Rachel should sound different, after all her long term partner had just died. David could not help thinking she sounded more frightened than upset. Maybe he was just reading too much in to the conversation but throughout the call her voice sounded fearful. Her insistence on him and Tom staying at the house was also odd. But then again maybe she just wanted to have some company. He decided not to pay too much attention to the nagging thoughts in his head and would address them again once he went back to Bristol. If he wanted to seek another opinion on the situation, then he would ask his friend, if he had an opinion.

He called Tom to give him the details of their trip.

"So we're gonna be staying at the house then? I hope I have my own bed cos I sure ain't sharing with you." Tom said.

"We could snuggle up and keep warm." David joked to his friend.

"What and feel your morning glory poking into my back at sun up? Keep dreaming pal! I have a reputation to maintain." Tom's retorts were always rapier fast.

"I'll have to pack a hot water bottle then."

"I'm hoping to pack a hot Bristol chick in through the back door when step mom isn't looking."

"She isn't my step-mother." David curtailed.

"As good as brethren as good as," Tom let the reprimand sail over his head.

"Ok. Well I'll catch you tomorrow."

"No problem chief. Sleep easy." With that Tom had hung up, not waiting for a reply.

Sleeping easy was not possible. Once David climbed into bed he was still thinking about the loss of a father he had only just started to know. Tom always insisted that you cannot miss what you did not have in the first place, but a father was different. Everybody had one, good or bad. And even if there was no living and breathing person to address as 'Dad', there was the idea of a father or father figure. David had just realised the feeling of having a father and within an instant that feeling was snatched away.

Sleep would eventually descend but not until after much tossing and turning. It was a disturbed and anxious slumber. Dark thoughts drifted through an already fatigued mind and denied any respite that the night had to offer, dark thoughts that were more than just bad dreams. Something felt very wrong.

Chapter Seven

"Are any of 'em right?" Billy asked, fearing the wrath of his brother.

Jimmy looked up from the table. The surface was covered with their haul from the previous night.

"None of 'em. Fuck it!" To be honest, Jimmy did not know what he was looking for exactly. A shotgun, ten gauge, about two hundred years old; an antique that was worth a few quid. That was as much as he knew.

The only person that knew the correct item was dead. Their ex-boss, John Hill, would have been the man to ask as it used to belong to him but since Hill had fallen from the top of his construction last week, that possibility had passed.

Jimmy knew that the shotgun had more value to Hill than it was actually worth. A couple of thousand pounds maybe, but not a figure worth dying over. There had to be another reason and maybe that was where the true value lay.

"What he want it for?" Billy asked.

The glare from his older brother was enough to tell Billy that he was not getting an answer; not a civil one at least. Billy knew that his brother was an angry man at the best of times but since they had been trying to retrieve the weapon, his anger had taken on a whole new level. Jimmy would rage over the simplest of things. He was not this angry when they lost their jobs at the construction site, just disappointed.

Also, Billy knew that his brother looked up to Hill almost like a father figure but not quite. Since their father had died, Jimmy seemed more at peace. Father; that was a joke, he was just the guy that both their mothers were sleeping with at the same time. The brothers were called the cousin brothers. Jimmy's mother was the elder sister of Billy's mother. They were both cousins and half-brothers. Such a stigma made their school life a difficult one. Kids can be cruel, and often are.

James Kinsella was a labourer and a part time criminal but not a very good one. He was charming and ruggedly good looking. Drinking, gambling and chasing women, was all he desired, along with money that he did not want to work for.

He had caught the eye of twenty year old Rose, a barmaid at his new local. Although his local would change frequently as he would always owe money to one of the regulars or he would be romancing the wrong women, which meant he would move on often.

Rose was young and naïve but a very pretty, natural blonde. She would always dress in short skirts to reveal her shapely legs and low cut tops to show off her ample cleavage. She was taken in by the smooth talking Kinsella, even though he was much older than her. He was tanned from working outdoors, tall and muscular. He had deep blue eyes, a flawless profile and salt & pepper dark hair.

After a few drinks, she stood no chance against his persuasive ways. Her virginity was taken in the rear alley of the pub, next to the empty kegs, once her shift had finished. Not only had she lost her virginity that night but she had also conceived her first child too, although that would not be known for a few months yet.

Kinsella thought he would stick around for a while as the sex was easy and the drinks were being served cost free. Rose even invited him home to meet her family, the staunchly Catholic Fegan clan. This is where he met her sixteen year old sister, Jane.

Jane was blessed with the same figure and exquisite Celtic good looks but she was a redhead. Kinsella had slept with all kinds of women in his years of hustling his way around the south west of England. Blondes, brunettes mostly, but he did have a thing for Oriental women. He loved their jet black hair, dark brown eyes and petit figures; at least all the ones he met were petit.

But as soon as he laid eyes on Jane with her long red hair, pale skin and pale green eyes; Irish beauty at its best, he had to have her. One night when Rose was working at the pub and Jane was babysitting for their younger brother, Kinsella turned up armed with a couple of bottles of wine. After just two glasses of wine and the slick talk of Kinsella, Jane gave herself to him on the family sofa.

Kinsella was living the dream for a few weeks. Publically courting the elder sister with all its obvious perks of free alcohol and repressed Catholic sexuality, while secretly seeing the very keen younger sister whenever he could.

The dream ended when Rose announced that she was pregnant. Kinsella never took precautions but he tried to do the right thing for once in his life and stuck around at least until the child was born. He even tried to end the affair with Jane but his weakness for the fairer sex overwhelmed him, frequently.

He offered to marry Rose after the birth but it was just a lame promise to keep her and the family sweet, a fact that he kept reiterating to Jane. She loved being the dark secret and her lack of maturity blinded her to this chancer's true intentions.

When the baby was born Kinsella insisted on the child having his name. So James Kinsella Junior was christened in a traditional Catholic ceremony just a few weeks after his birth. Although, the child was never called James, only ever Jimmy.

Jane had hidden her other dark secret from Kinsella as well as her family. She wore baggy clothes to cover her gaining weight and had told her lover that they should cool it while her nephew was born and being christened but it was just part of her desperation to cover her own pregnancy.

The inevitable happened and the secret was out. Her waters broke one morning before school. She gave birth eight weeks prematurely to William Francis Fegan, just two months after Jimmy's birth.

Kinsella disappeared overnight. He had left his flat and the labouring job he was barely holding down. No word. No forwarding address.

The situation nearly destroyed the family. The sisters did not speak for a few years and the cousins/brothers did not spend their early years together. Rose did not believe that Kinsella would betray her like that and that he had only slept with the young sister because Jane had seduced him. Rose moved out of the family home to live just a few streets away from her family, but it could have been the other side of the world for the amount of contact she had with them.

Once on her own, Kinsella returned briefly but only for whatever he could get from the now vulnerable Rose. After a few weeks of rent free sex he was gone.

The sisters eventually regained contact because the boys started at the same school, at the same time such was the closeness in their age. The feud thawed as the young Jimmy and Billy were drawn together and played with each other unaware of the relationship between them. The teachers were also oblivious to the family connection with the boys having different surnames and encouraged them in their obvious friendship.

Even though the sisters eventually reinvigorated their relationship for the sake of their boys, there was still a distance between Rose and her parents because they favoured young Billy over her son. The resentment she held was unintentionally fostered in Jimmy. The boys were very different in personality and aptitude, Jimmy being smart and shrewd yet angry and troublesome, and Billy was of a softer nature but dense at the same time. Even from junior school, Jimmy was the far more dominant sibling and his brother would be easily manipulated into trouble. The only similarities they had was the good looking rugged genes of their father, their shared DNA obvious apart from Jimmy having his mother's dirty blond hair and Billy the red hair of his.

When word got round that they were the product of an illicit encounter between one man and two sisters, the rumour mill made up its own stories. When they hit secondary school, where the cruel kids were far more cruel, the tales of their conception became vastly exaggerated. With creative accounts of incestuous group sex that involved other family members and that included the family's pet dog.

Jimmy dealt out his own kind of vengeance with viscous beatings outside of school hours. Billy was always there to back up the slightly older brother who seemed to be protecting him against the taunts. And after several violent events in carparks, playgrounds and sports fields spread over a couple of years, the boys had earned themselves fierce reputation; a reputation which extended beyond their own borough and brought the teenage scrappers from far and wide to their door. Once they had established themselves as ruthless fighters, fearless against all comers, the taunting stopped. Although the nickname, the cousin brothers did stick. There was no denying this as they were both cousins, and brothers. Those formative trials as teenagers had bonded them in ways that mere siblings would never experience.

Twenty years or so later the two were still inseparable. The violently fragmented upbringing fused them as one.

Chapter Eight

Tom made their trip to Bristol an event. He picked David up early and took him for a large greasy breakfast at a local layby café. There was a selection of David's favourite music in the glove compartment, a copy of The Sun and a big bag of sweets. The car was an old beaten up Vauxhall Astra but Tom had even washed it for the trip. The washing had just revealed a rust hole and several stone chips that were previously covered by the mud that had caked the car for the last couple of months.

"You've washed the car. I'm honoured!" David said as they got back into the car after their calorie rich breakfast. He had not noticed until they were sitting in the café waiting for food to arrive and staring at the car, trying to figure out what was different.

"I got a new air freshener as well if you didn't notice?" Tom replied.

"I thought it was that cheap ass aftershave you buy."

"When I have my winning looks and personality, I don't need the expensive crap like you wear." All insults were delivered with a brotherly love. "Besides, we may get lucky in Bristol. I know I will, but you might too if you get them drunk enough."

"I won't be looking for any hook ups." David said.

Tom turned the key but he had to try the ignition three times before the engine fired.

"Of course you won't. Why change the habit of a lifetime?" Tom was referring to the fact that David had not been in a relationship for some time. He was never looking for female company, even on a night out.

"I'm sure there won't be any opportunity for that. We'll go for a meal with Rachel tonight. The funeral is tomorrow and we come back the next day. See, there won't be any time for much else." David reiterated the planned itinerary.

"Whatever Cochise!" A love of too many Bruce Willis films was apparent from the creative nicknames Tom had for all his associates.

They pulled out of the layby and joined the flow of traffic. Tom opened the glove compartment and pulled out a CD box. It always frustrated David that he would only change the CD whilst the car was in motion. Two minutes previously the car had been stationary but Tom would never think to make the musical selection from the safety of a parking bay.

The sound of some early U2 came through the speakers. The volume was at a moderate level because like the rest of the dilapidated car, the speakers would crackle over a certain volume. They enjoyed some comfortable silences with the music playing. Anything that filtered out of the speakers became the soundtrack to their journey.

What would start as the closure of a distressing chapter of David's life would open up a whole new sphere of his life; some good, some bad.

Chapter Nine

Jones sat in the car waiting in the small rear carpark. The Gunroom was a store that while selling all kinds of hunting and shotgun related items, also had dealings with some specialist and antique weaponry. The owner, Duncan Bailey, was a wealthy man with a passion for firearms but he also had links with some of the local criminal gangs.

The lights in the upstairs office flicked off. Jones had been watching Bailey for some time now and had his routine down. Not because of this job but just because Bailey had a finger in so many pies that eventually he would be the missing piece in somebody's jigsaw. Jones figured this could be the right call.

Every Thursday night Bailey would stay late to process a replenishment delivery and with a local shoot coming up, he would take the opportunity to supply the ammunition at a discount, but not so much of a reduction that he would be out of pocket and not so little that he couldn't make any sales. The event would also raise his profile with the local hobnobs and make his business appear to be a higher brow operation than it actually was.

The truth was that Bailey used to supply the shotguns and firearms for any robbery jobs that were happening in the area. That was twenty plus years ago when he was the 'go-to' guy who could get you what you needed but never asked questions. If you needed shotguns, handguns, ammo, a clean vehicle and even drivers; Bailey was the man to go see. His whole business was built on dirty money.

Jones stepped out of the car. He already had his gloves on. The best place for him to stand was on the corner, away from the rear CCTV camera. Many places had dummy cameras but to the experienced eye you could tell the difference and these were the real McCoy; Infrared PIR, night vision and HDD recording. A man that still has to look over his shoulder from years of unlawful activities paid to have the best money could buy. Bailey had the best.

In the darkness Jones could hear the clipping footsteps of a man wearing expensive shoes coming down the stairs to the rear exit. The door opened. Escaping light from the corridor illuminated the small delivery bay. Jones looked away as not to have the light effect his vision. His eyes had become accustomed to the darkness which Bailey's would not. This was an advantage that he did not really need. He had the element of surprise. He was younger, fitter and stronger than Bailey. But also he was conscience free and motivated.

The light was flicked off and the carpark was bathed in darkness once more. Jones heard the door slam and the beeping of the security code being punched into the backlit panel to the right of the door. Jones had surveyed this area over the last few days and knew the minor details.

The alarm tone changed from a solid tone to a series of shorts beeps until there was a final double beep indicating that the alarm was set. The next sound was the popping of the locks from Bailey's Land Rover Discovery. It was a high end model with personalised plates, just the type of vehicle you needed when rubbing shoulders with rich rural types at grouse shooting events.

As Bailey stepped around the corner, keys in one hand and briefcase in the other, he was not expecting to have a muscular arm taut around his neck or to feel the cold steel of a blade in the dark against his skin.

"Walk or die?" It was a question and a statement together. Jones never uttered more words than he needed to.

"Huh?" It was not really an answer but a resignation.

Jones walked the overweight man to the darkest corner of the carpark where there was a black BMW. Even in the dim light Bailey could see that the car had no visible number plates. They had either been removed or obscured as not to show up on CCTV. The boot of the saloon was already open with plastic sheeting laid across the floor.

"Drop your things in."

Bailey did as he was told. He dropped the large bunch of keys and leather case onto the plastic. At this point it could have been a robbery, Bailey thought. But he was so wrong.

His hands were pulled behind him and some pre-prepared cable tie cuffs were applied very tightly to his wrists. A vicious shove saw the big man fall on top of his things face down. More cable ties were placed onto his ankles.

"W-what do you want? I-I have money!" Bailey protested.

There was no reply. Jones heaved Bailey's head back by pulling on his long greying hair. Two six inch pieces of duct tape was applied to the man's mouth and he was silenced. Jones took the keys from the boot and slammed the tailgate shut.

Bailey whimpered in the darkness. He had waited for something like this to happen for years but was so unprepared now that it had actually happened. From the isolated void he could hear his abductor walking across the carpark and get in the Discovery. He did not want to think about what would happen next, but lying bound and gagged on plastic was the nightmare setting of too many gangster movies. The plastic was not for blood as Bailey thought, it was for would happen next. His anxiety got the better of him and Bailey urinated himself; the humiliating side of fear.

Chapter Ten

"Duncs ain't answering." Billy said.

"Try him later, but make sure you do." Jimmy always scolded. He always expected to be disappointed by his brother. There would often be a reprimand but never praise for the younger sibling.

"What are we gonna do with all these guns til then?"

"Wrap em up, tie em up and stick em in the shed. Don't be seen!"

Billy started the slow process of wrapping the guns in newspaper and parcel tape. He would later wrap them in bin bags and bundle them into an old army kit bag to be dropped into the secret lock box they had hidden under their garden shed. The shed had a false floor which looked like it was solid but when lifted it had a trap door that was above a sunken lock box buried beneath. It had proved to be quite a successful hiding place for illegal items in the past.

"Where do you suppose he is?" Billy asked.

"How the fuck do I know?" Jimmy rebuked.

They had a long history with Duncan Bailey. Jimmy used to drive on some of the jobs that Bailey provided for. Jimmy was a good driver although he had never passed a driving test. He had a driving license but somebody else had taken the test for him, again arranged by Bailey. The brothers also used to be hired as security for some of the bigger events that Bailey held once he started to go into legitimate business ventures.

Bailey had been good to the boys over the years. He had found them real employment when they needed it and gave them some cash-in-hand jobs every now and again. The truth was Bailey liked to use the brothers because they were reliable and ruthless. Jimmy was a shrewd operator but brutally violent. Billy was intensely loyal to his brother and would do anything to please his elder sibling regardless of what it was. Billy even changed his surname from Fegan to Kinsella to be more like his brother.

Their first meeting with Bailey had been when the boys were just teenagers. The brothers were scraping a living from shoplifting, burglary and some drug dealing. Their plan was to steal items to order from the larger retailers for some of the other local felons, and break into a few houses to pawn whatever valuables they could. With the money made they would visit one of the many local drug dealers and come to an agreement. They would provide protection and collection services in exchange for cut price pills and weed, which they could in turn sell on for a profit. It was turning out an income of a few hundred pounds a week for the lads, neither of which had reached their eighteenth birthday at the time.

They had made a mistake and decided to break into a large house just outside the city in the dead of night. The house looked like there was nobody home, there were no dogs inside and no sign of a burglar alarm system; easy pickings, or so the brothers had thought.

Entry was made through the garage. A crowbar wedged under the front edge of the flimsy metal door popped the lock easy. Once inside, a glass panel door is all that stood between them and the rest of the house. Jimmy smashed the glass and carefully reached a hand through to unlock the door. The plan was to start upstairs and work their way down. Jewellery and bundles of money always seemed to be stashed upstairs in big houses or so Jimmy thought and so they set to work.

The boys were ransacking the main bedroom when a van and two cars pulled up the drive. One of Billy's mistakes that night was to leave the garage door half open thus alerting the returning owner to the intruder's presence.

By the time the boys had noticed they had been rumbled, the occupants of the three vehicles were all in the house. Bailey had been on a robbery instead of just supplying the necessary weaponry and man power. He had a big crew with him as the job that night was raiding a large wholesale depot in the city. The target items were cigarettes, alcohol and any cash, all of which had been dropped at a lock up. The gang had come back to the house to get paid for the nights work.

Jimmy came down the staircase to be greeted by Bailey, flanked by five men. Two had baseball bats, one a crowbar. Billy made an entrance at the top of the stairs and waited to see what his brother would do.

Anybody would be forgiven for pleading stupidity and trying to leave the house with their tail between their legs with a thick ear or bloody nose. Not Jimmy, he was fearless.

In one swift action, Jimmy punched the closest man in the face. The man went down hard and released his weapon. Jimmy kicked out at the knee of the next man who also dropped to the floor writhing in agony as his leg had been bent the wrong way. As the other men responded to the attack Billy launched himself down the stairs and into the melee.

The brothers traded blows with the remaining men until they were eventually overwhelmed and beaten down to the floor. Jimmy still tried to fight even with blood pouring from a gash in his head and a broken nose. Both injuries were caused by a baseball bat. Billy was unconscious after a blow from the crowbar. Many an older and harder man would have stayed down but Jimmy would not quit.

"Give it up son." Bailey said with admiration for the young lad.

"Fuck You!" Spat the blood streaked Jimmy.

"Your pal is down and so will you be soon, give it up." Bailey's words were not harsh but fair.

Jimmy looked down at his stricken brother. If he was unconscious, or worse killed, then there would be nobody to protect Billy. The older man was right.

"You pair have some stones! Who are you?" Bailey asked.

There was no need to lie or resist anymore. They were caught.

"I'm Jimmy. This is my brother Billy." His voice was still filled with confrontation.

"Take it easy boy. " Bailey raised his hand as a gesture of truce. "What's your last name?"

"Kinsella."

"I've heard of you." He could see the surprise in the young man's eyes "The Cousin Brothers!"

Jimmy said nothing he just stared angrily at the man before him, then down at his brother again who was starting to stir.

"Jay, fix these two up." Bailey nodded toward the boys. "Clean em up. Get them something to eat and drink and then I'm gonna have a chat with em."

One of the men helped Jimmy off his knees and together they picked up Billy. Once the brothers and the other injured men had been given some rudimentary medical attention, Bailey made Jimmy an offer.

Bailey could see that he could help mould these two young protégées into valuable assets in his criminal dealings. As it happened, over time Jimmy would become his right hand man. They say there is no honour among thieves but there was mutual respect. He treated the boys like his own sons and they, in turn, substituted Bailey for their absent father. Twenty years later they still had that bond.

Chapter Eleven

The trip had been a stop start affair. Tom constantly drank high caffeine soft drinks which resulted in multiple toilet breaks, but they eventually got to Bristol. The roads were busy at any time of day in a big city but they had arrived at around lunchtime which seemed to add to the congestion. They were heading for a flat in the Clifton area of the city so needed to pass through the worst of the city centre traffic.

The apartment was in a large four storey period house that had been split into three separate dwellings. David's father had owned the whole building but rented out the ground and first floor apartments while living above in the largest of the three which took up the second and third floors.

Rachel was there to meet them as they arrived. She was not planning to go back to work until after the funeral, as was to be expected when a partner dies. But she also worked in the site office of the construction site where John Hill had met his death. If she was being honest with herself she may never go back.

The friends climbed out of the car almost simultaneously but while David climbed the wide steps to hug Rachel, Tom merely stretched his stiff limbs and surveyed his new surroundings, mostly the girlfriend of his friend's dead father. Rachel was of average height and had the figure that was a perfect balance between curvy and slim. David had told Tom previously that his father had met her when she worked in a pole dancing club. That gave Tom a preconceived idea of what she was like before they were even introduced.

After what David felt was an uncomfortably long embrace with his father's bereaved partner, he introduced Rachel to Tom. She also hugged Tom. David could see the bemusement on his friends face over Rachel's shoulder. Once she released him, again after a longer time than was necessary, she led them up to the flat.

The building was old but in an excellent restored condition. The staircases were that bit wider than what would be found in a modern building. The doors were also wider and the ceilings taller. It was an impressive building with all the character that would be expected from a property of that age but with modern attributes. Expensive rugs covered the high gloss varnished wooden hallway. Stylish contemporary artwork hung from the old picture rails that were only present in a house this period.

The apartment had an open plan kitchen/diner/lounge arrangement. The kitchen was styled in high quality wooden units and a marble worktop with the window looking over a small contained paved and decked garden. The lounge seating area was towards the front of the building to make the best use of the large bay windows, two large sofas and coffee table faced a flat screen TV affixed to the wall. A large rustic dining table separated the two areas but perfectly complimented both, creating a truly cosy and functional living space.

"Make yourself at home and I'll put the kettle on." Rachel said. Her voice cracked like she either had a cold or had been crying recently. The latter was more understandable under the circumstances.

"You don't have to…" David started.

"A coffee, milk and two would be great. Thank you." Tom interrupted.

Rachel pottered off to the other side of the large open space to make the drinks.

"Can't you see she's upset?" David reprimanded in a hushed tone.

"She probably wants to keep busy. You do when…you know…people…." Tom tried to pick his words carefully but failed "…die."

"Tea, David?" Rachel asked from the kitchen.

He responded with a yes as she was already making a drink for Tom. David looked around the room and noticed a new picture on the wall. It was a photo of him and his father from a meal out. David had treated his father and Rachel to a night in the local Indian restaurant. Rachel had taken a picture on her phone. The family resemblance was easy to see. So alike in looks but different in so many other ways.

"How old was your dad?" Tom asked in a whisper.

"Fifty-six, why?"

"And how old is she?" Again in a whisper but gesturing towards Rachel as she had her back turned against the conversation.

"Thirty-two...thirty-three, something like that," David answered.

"Ding dong! Your dad was the man." Tom's tone, although low, was one of admirable insinuation. Rachel was an attractive woman for a man of any age but for a much older man there was laddish kudos to give in light of a twenty plus year age gap.

Rachel placed the drinks on wooden coasters on the wooden coffee table that matched all the other wooden items.

"How long have you lived here?" Tom asked trying to sound like he was making small talk.

"I moved in here with John about eight years ago." She then returned to the kitchen to bring in her own coffee.

Tom raised his hands to the ceiling and mouthed a silent 'Wow!' at the revelation that his friend's father would have been twice the age of his girlfriend when she first moved in and the kudos points had just doubled. David elbowed Tom in the ribs as Rachel turned back towards the friends.

"What do you want to do tonight? Takeaway, restaurant or I can cook if you prefer?" She asked them. Her voice shook as she spoke.

"Don't go to any trouble Rachel. And maybe a restaurant isn't appropriate under the circumstances. I'll grab a takeaway for us all later, if you like?" David offered.

"That sounds good to me." She smiled the first smile since they arrived. Rachel had one of those faces that would be transformed by a smile. She was at best naively pretty when expressionless but her cheekbones would lift and her eyes would shine when she broke a smile. Also her cheeks were dimpled but the most significant change was to the width of her mouth and the perfectly straight white teeth that were revealed.

"Chinese or Indian?" Tom interjected.

"Chinese!" Rachel and David said simultaneously. They looked at each other and grinned. Rachel grinned for longer than David.

Chapter Twelve

Jimmy was started to feel a little anxious regards the whereabouts of Bailey. There was nobody to miss him apart from the brothers. Bailey's wife had left him years ago due to his criminal connections and he never saw his daughter since she had moved to Australia.

The only other person that would question his absence was old Bob that worked part time at The Gunroom. Bob only worked a few days to help out with the delivery and on a Saturday. Bailey rarely took time off these days. He would make an effort for a special shooting event and have an early finish but days off were unheard of. The store was closed on a Sunday and luckily that would be when most the events would be. Bob was part of the furniture. Seventy-three years old and never wanted to retire, Bob would probably die at the store. But this week Bob was away visiting his sick sister up in Lancashire.

Jimmy was feeling tense. He had sent Billy out for some milk and bread but he wanted his younger brother to go via Bailey's house and then the store. Just in case the man they looked to as a father had turned up.

The front door opened and Billy staggered in with a load of shopping bags. Jimmy watched his brother struggle in while sitting at the kitchen table, coffee in one hand, a cigarette in the other.

"Bread and milk! That's all we needed. What the fuck have you bought?" Every conversation was in some way a criticism of his brother.

"They had some offers on beer. I thought we could get…." Billy tried to explain.

"Fuck that! Did you find Duncs?" The interruption was harsh and aggressive.

"He wasn't there, Jimmy. Not the house, nor the store." The younger brother knew the information would not be received well.

"Did you see his car?" Jimmy knew he would have to drag the details out.

Billy looked sheepish and shook his head.

"Anything else?" The older sibling asked with a heavy dose of sarcasm in his voice.

"The store was shut."

Jimmy knew that Bob was away. The sister was older than Bob and suffering from cancer with not much time left.

"Fuck it!" The rage filled his face as he took a long hard pull on his diminishing cigarette. He stubbed out the butt and pulled his phone from his pocket. The finger taps on the screen were much firmer than was necessary.

"Who you calling Jimmy?" Billy had not learned to keep his mouth shut when the red mist descended over his brother.

"SHUT UP!!!"

Jimmy slammed the mobile down on to the table as Bailey's phone went to answer phone yet again. The mobile did not break that time but Jimmy went through a lot of phones due to his temper.

"Was the funeral today?" Billy had a flash of inspiration and pulled a nugget of information from the depths of his subservient brain. John Hill was being buried this week but the date escaped him.

"No. It's tomorrow. Perhaps we'll pay that slag Rachel a visit." Jimmy did not like Rachel because she had knocked him back when she was still pole dancing. He had always liked her before she was with Hill. He liked her tight dancer's curves and the way she kept her hair bobbed and dyed red. She was a looker alright. And now she was single again.

"Will she know where Duncs is Jimmy?"

There was no answer to that question just a shaking of his head, not as 'No' but in disbelief in the stupidity of his brother. He drained the rest of his coffee and lit another cigarette.

"Put that shit away and then fuck off and leave me alone." There would be no more conversation until it was time to leave. And they would leave when it was dark. Jimmy believed that people got scared in the dark and it would make them talk more easily. People were scared of Jimmy whether it was dark or not.

Chapter Thirteen

The air was musty and dank. Water could be heard dripping somewhere. The sound echoed within the hollow walls of the derelict building. But that was the only sound Bailey could hear.

He had awoken from a very disturbed and uncomfortable slumber. The chair he was tied to was hard. His lower limbs felt heavy and lifeless through lack of movement. A sack now covered his head and the tape was still in place. The cable ties cut deeply into his wrists, all the struggling in the boot of the car had been a mistake. They were designed to tighten under resistance and tighten they did, he couldn't feel his fingers as the blood could no longer flow into them.

The fear and isolation of the situation made him weep. He was not violent unless he had to be, as criminals go, he was quite a placid man. Self-defence was one thing but abduction and incarceration was something else. He had no concept of time which added to his confusion. He could make out natural light so assumed it was daytime but it could be early morning or the middle of the day. He may never know.

All he did know was that the man who took him had left while it was still dark. Bailey could not even guess where he was being held. The journey in the boot had so many stops and starts with the car being parked up in various places that he was clueless as to any possible location. But if he was being honest with himself, his whereabouts was the least of his worries.

Somewhere beyond the walls he could hear a car approaching but not by the sound of the engine. The tyres must have been throwing up grit and all kinds of other debris. The sound seemed to encircle the building. As the vehicle drew closer, Bailey knew it was the BMW he had unceremoniously travelled in. His heart started to beat rapidly with the anticipation of what was to come but the blood still could not get to his extremities.

The car stopped. The crunching and pinging of debris stopped and the only sound was the low thrum of the engine, interrupted momentarily by the constant slow drip of water, a leak that would never be fixed.

The engine was now silenced and a car door could be heard opening, then slamming shut. The debris started to move again but this time by footsteps. The boot could be heard being opened and then after a moment, that was slammed too. More crunching of what must have been broken glass and crumbling concrete underfoot as the footsteps drew closer, each one counting down to the crucial moment; the moment of what would happen next.

The footsteps stopped directly in front of Bailey. There was a sound of something being placed on to the ground. The sack was lifted from his face. The dim light still hurt his eyes after hours of darkness from the sack.

Bailey's eyes focussed on the figure before him. The man wore a decorator's coverall with a hood, and a mask attached on a length of elastic. In his hand was a piece of steel pipe.

He was clearly an athletically built man and although not much of his face was exposed, what was on show was craggy and grizzled. On the floor was a strange yellow plastic box with a carry handle. It took a minute for Bailey to fully take in what stood before him but the yellow box was something he had seen before in the medical tent at an event recently. It was a portable defibrillator unit.

The man dropped the mask, and the full horror of his situation hit Bailey like both barrels of a shotgun. He knew who this man was, and worse, he knew what would come next.

Chapter Fourteen

After another round of coffee and tea and some awkward conversation, Rachel showed the friends to their rooms for the night. Tom was in the small guest bedroom-come-office on the second floor. David was in the main guest room in the attic space where he had stayed before. He had revealed to Tom that his room was directly opposite his father's room and on one of his previous visits he had heard Rachel and his father having sex. A fact that David prayed Tom would not bring up after a drink or two with Rachel present.

David had said that they would give Rachel some space and the two men decided to spend a few hours in their own rooms. Tom would always try and catch some sleep if he was at a loose end. Resting from being in such a high energy state, he would say.

David grabbed a paperback from his holdall and lay onto the bed. He wanted some space to gather his thoughts for the funeral tomorrow. There would be a wake afterwards with his father's work colleagues and what family he had left. The thought of interacting with strangers at the most intimate of family gatherings was not a situation David was looking forward to at all. That is why he had brought Tom with him, someone to help him out of tricky conversations and to keep him away from trouble. Trouble had a habit of finding David.

He was lost in a story of crime and intrigue by Jeffery Deaver when the door opened. Rachel walked in dressed in an oversized white towelling bathrobe.

"I've brought you some towels." She sat on the corner of the bed and placed a stack of white towels next to her. They were folded in a way they make David think either Rachel had OCD or at some time she used to work in a hotel.

"Thank you." David rolled over to face her. He sensed that she was going to say more.

"No problem. If you want anything, please just ask." She said with an uncomfortable smile.

"Ok." David did not want to engage her in any conversation. There was something not right. Yes, she should be upset but something else was going on here. He would help her anyway he could but it was what she might ask that made him nervous.

"I'm gonna have a shower now and a lie down. You're more than welcome to use my en suite if you don't want to go down to the main bathroom."

"Thanks Rachel." He smiled his own uncomfortable smile.

She touched him on the leg as if to form some kind of connection and then left suddenly without another word.

David rolled back onto his stomach and tried to read the book again but he stared blankly at the words as if they were in Japanese. When he heard how his father had fallen from the building it felt all wrong. Not because his recently found father was now dead, but because he had formed a bond and had gotten to know his father's personality quite well in a very short space of time. John Hill did not seem like the kind of man that would take risks at work. He came across as a very fastidious organizer and played everything by the book. How a man of this type fell from a building on a calm sunny day seemed beyond him. He was not convinced that it was an accident.

The sound of the shower being switched on in the room opposite distracted him from the disturbing train of thought he was engaging in. He had not noticed that Rachel left his door ajar.

He hopped off the bed to shut the door and then realised that the door to Rachel's room was also wide open, giving David a clear line of sight into the en suite bathroom. Rachel stood naked with her back to the door. The evidence of her dancing was obvious. Her slim athletic figure shown in all its glory by the flawless tanned skin that was now on show for David to gaze upon. He slowly shut the door but could not take his eyes off her while he pulled it closed. He had not seen a naked woman in quite a few months but this was one woman he should not be looking at, with or without any desire to do so. He fell back onto the bed and picked the book back up. After a few pages he fell into a deep restful sleep. He needed it

Chapter Fifteen

It did not matter that Bailey said he would talk. It did not matter that he pleaded not to be harmed. It did not even matter if Bailey had produced the item that Jones was after. Jones was still going to kill him anyway.

He would not take the chance that Bailey would keep his mouth shut afterwards. Bailey was a criminal, no matter how much he tried to distance himself from the past. Anybody who had dealings of an illicit nature that required some outside help, would either directly or indirectly involve associates of Bailey. This man had had his fingers in too many criminal pies for so long the stigma was hard to shake. Jones peeled the tape from Bailey's mouth.

"What do you want?" Bailey's voice trembled.

"Mortimer 10 gauge Hammer Gun." Jones answered the question.

"What?" He was perplexed. "If you need a gun, I can get you a gun. I wouldn't charge you or anyth...."

"I have a gun." Jones pulled the Glock from inside the decorator's coverall while interrupting the terrified man.

"P-please don't shoot me!" Bailey pleaded.

"Don't worry Duncan; I'm not going to shoot you." There was no comfort in the tone of voice that delivered that sentence.

"Y-you're not?"

"A bullet would look like murder. Murder is too good for you." There was a smile but a malevolent one.

"Please….I have money. I'll pay you." Bailey was desperate.

"So does my employer." Jones was starting to tire of the conversation. "A Mortimer 10 gauge Hammer Gun, do you have it?"

"I-I c-can get you one."

"I don't want you to acquire one for me. If I did I would have come to your store and asked for one. There was one, recently in the possession of an associate of yours, John Hill. I want that one."

The penny dropped. Bailey had known Hill for years. They had had many dealing together both legal and illegal. He was supposed to attend Hill's funeral that week. But now it was clear that Hill had not fallen from the building in an accident. Bailey had always suspected that maybe there was more to it. He knew Hill wanted out, the only problem with that was Hill's business was essential to the organisation; a fact that Bailey had been openly jealous about.

"I d-don't have his…!" He knew that was the wrong answer.

"Who does?"

"I don't know. It was stolen, w-weeks ago," if Bailey was not scared before, he was really scared now. He knew that the shotgun had gone missing. It was an antique that Hill had been given years ago. Why did this man want it? The weapon was deactivated and could not be fired. Also, it was not worth much at all, a couple of grand at the most. Either Hill had been killed for it or because of it. The only question was why?

"That's a shame." Jones reached into his coverall and pulled out a lock knife. He put the Glock away.

"W-what are you going to do?" Bailey's head swivelled as Jones walked behind him.

The hired man reached down and grabbed the makeshift handcuffs made from cable ties. The razor sharp knife easily cut through the tough plastic bindings.

Bailey pulled his hands in front of him and looked at where the ties had marked his wrists. There were two red rings around the wrist joints but no broken skin. Jones pulled out the gun again and handed Bailey the knife.

"Free your ankles." Jones' tone was neutral. The previous malice was gone.

The older overweight man did as he was told. For a nanosecond he thought about attacking Jones with the knife but with the gun pointing at him, it would have been a futile action.

Jones held out his left hand. Bailey passed back the knife. The two men stood looking at each other for a moment.

"Are you letting me go?"

"Do you want me to let you?" It was a cruel question.

"Um…Yeah!" Bailey hesitated.

"Under the chair."

Bailey looked behind him. Underneath where he was sitting was a magazine. Bailey was confused.

"Pick it up and thumb to page 36." Jones said casually.

Bailey did as he was told. The publication was a fetish magazine. Every page had naked men or women bound and gagged. Some of the images showed torture fantasy, sadism and more disturbing scenes that Bailey skipped over. A man was tied to an 'X' shaped cross while a masked woman dress in PVC whipped him, blood ran down his back. Page 36 had an overweight man, his hands cable tied together behind him, exactly as Bailey had been, sat on a chair while a dominatrix humiliated him.

"What is this?" Bailey asked.

"If you were discovered before I returned then a story of abduction would be harder to prove if you were badged as a fat, old pervert."

The words stung Bailey. He was known for weekend trips into the red light district and paying top price for a high end hooker on special occasions like Christmas and his birthday.

Jones put away the knife and the gun then took the magazine in his gloved hand. He gestured toward the doorway. Bailey had been so preoccupied looking at Jones, the magazine and waiting to see what would happen next, that he had not taken any notice of where he was. The building was a derelict factory or industrial unit of some kind. There was a doorframe with no door whatsoever at the far side of the large room.

Bailey slowly walked towards the doorway but he kept glancing back at Jones, who was following him and keeping pace.

"Are you really letting me go?" Bailey asked.

"What do you think?"

"I'm not sure." Bailey could now taste the fresh air as he neared the doorway, although the dank stench of the unused building still filled his nostrils.

The daylight was almost blinding. Jones' black BMW was parked in the middle of a parking area that could have parked a dozen cars. The lines painted onto the tarmac the designate the spaces had all but faded. At the far side of the building, there was an enclosed shed. Inside was Bailey's White Range Rover.

"The keys are in it." Jones said as he noticed the relieved man's eyes spot the vehicle.

Bailey walked toward the shed, again slowly and again Jones' followed him.

As the two men entered the shed, Bailey turned to Jones.

"Why are you following me?"

"Just in case you have a hidden weapon and you tried to shoot me." Jones said deadpan.

"Oh...ok. I don't have any guns." Bailey reached for the driver's side door and opened it.

"I know." Jones threw the magazine into the car as a distraction. Swiftly, Jones got behind the large man and applied a sleeper hold. With a crook of his arm forming a vice like grip around the other man's neck, Jones pulled back firmly but not with too much pressure. Bailey's arms flailed around in a moment of panic. He desperately tried to break the younger man's hold but the task was impossible. Quickly, Bailey succumbed to the lack of oxygen flowing to his brain and slumped against his aggressor.

Jones pushed the unconscious man in through the driver's door, having to lift Bailey's legs to get the whole body into the car.

"I didn't want to carry your fat ass out here." Jones said to the unhearing slumped figure in the car. He walked back to the building to retrieve the defibrillator. Bailey was old and overweight. It was about time he had himself a heart attack. Jones was going to make sure of that.

Chapter Sixteen

There was something satisfying about taking the plastic off a new pack of cigarettes and pulling out the silver paper to reveal twenty fresh virgin smokes. Jimmy took one and placed in between his lips. He savoured the fresh sweet smell of the tobacco as it escaped from the open pack. He would keep these small pleasures to himself. Everybody knew about his big pleasures, women, drink, smokes and money; not necessarily in that order.

He sparked his Zippo lighter and pulled a huge lung full of nicotine infused smoke from the cigarette.

"When are we gonna go out?" Billy spoiled the moment.

"Later. Shut it!" Jimmy snarled.

"Are we gonna see Ducty?" Billy was referring to Steve 'Ducty' Allen, a cannabis grower and distributor. Ducty was so called because when he was seventeen years old he was beaten up by one of the local gangs for selling his weed on their patch. The final insult after the severe beating was the gang duct taped Allen naked to the fire escape staircase on one of the rougher estates. He had been gagged to keep him silent and when he was found he was hypothermic and delirious. A bunch of school kids had found him and had taken pictures on mobile phones for trophies before calling somebody to cut him down. He was called the Duct Tape kid for some time afterwards but that was eventually shortened to Ducty. That was fifteen odd years ago.

"Maybe, now shut up.!"

The brothers sat in silence. The remains of a high calorie lunch, cooked by Billy, lay on the plates before them. Billy would also have to wash up. The more dominant brother did very little if he could help it. For now Billy could sit in silence as that is what Jimmy wanted.

Jimmy's phone vibrated on the kitchen table. He picked it up in his large thick fingers and answered the call. He did not recognise the number.

"Yeah!" It was as polite as he would ever be on the phone.

Billy could hear the mumbling voice at the other end of the phone. It sounded like a man's voice to him. He did not know all of his brother contacts.

"What? Where?"

More mumbling, Jimmy's face became red with rage. He hung up the phone.

"What is it?" Billy dare ask.

"Duncs' car has been found." Jimmy got his feet and reached for the car keys.

"Where we going?" Billy asked.

His brother did not answer him. Jimmy pulled on his jacket and headed for the door. Billy knew this meant that he should follow and keep the questions to a minimum. He did just that.

Chapter Seventeen

Pete 'The Pikey' Flynn drove his Mercedes Sprinter slowly out of the Severn Gate Site. He had found a few bits and pieces that might be worth a few quid but either nobody was dumping on the site anymore or he had been beaten to the good stuff. The only significant find was Duncan Bailey's Land Rover. He did not approach the vehicle but he knew the registration plate and who it belonged to.

Flynn had only called Jimmy Kinsella out of courtesy. It was also a favour he could call in at a later date. Flynn did not like the Kinsellas much but their reputation was so brutal that he would prefer to be on the right side of them. Nothing really scared Flynn but he had respect for Jimmy but only in so much that Jimmy was one of the few men that could trade blows and hold his own with the best of the bare knuckle underclass. 'The enemy of my enemy is my friend' was Flynn's mantra and their mutual enemy was the law.

The van cruised at a very low speed. Flynn scanned the hedges and along grass for anything that might have value. There would always be an old bicycle, a pallet or some scrap metal dumped somewhere along disused roads like this one.

He caught something out of the corner of his eye. Just parked off the road, but hidden in a narrow overgrown dirt track in a secluded layby, was a black car. Opportunity knocks every now and then. Flynn thought that maybe this would be one of those moments. There could be valuables in the car or there might be someone in the car doing something they shouldn't. He had caught a few doggers in his time and he liked to watch the action. One time he had scored a blow job off some posh middle aged lady who was servicing all comers. When you frequent the darker areas of society you meet a class of people that have a darker and conscience free lifestyle. Flynn was deep within that kind of existence.

He pulled up directly in front of the car which he could see was a new model BMW. The car looked empty but a closer look was needed. Flynn reached for a crowbar he kept tucked behind his seat and stepped out of the van. In his pocket was a small LED torch. He pulled it out and cast a beam over the front seats. Empty.

As he circled the car he could hear the engine tapping from cooling down. The car had only just been parked here which would mean that the occupants might not be too far away. The car looked empty of valuables. Not even a few coins in the drinks holder, which was common. The car was spotless, like it had just been valeted.

If he broke a window the alarm might go off. He kicked the car to see if there was an alarm; nothing. It was unusual for a new BMW not to have an alarm. He tried the door; locked.

Flynn walked around the car again. Something was wrong with this situation but until somebody turned up and told him any different he would still treat the vehicle as a find that he could profit from. He would take the alloys, if nothing else.

He returned to the van and slid open the roadside payload door. In the back there were various tools, jacks and more importantly locking wheel nut adapters for a variety of vehicles. Alloys could be worth anything to a fence but more if they could be sold on eBay. Flynn was illiterate so technology was not an option for him and he could see a wad of cash to the tune of £300 for quick sale on a set of near pristine BMW alloys. More, if he bartered harder.

He dropped his crowbar into the tool box and grabbed a tyre iron and a handful of wheel nut adapters. One was bound to fit.

As he turned to jump down from the van, he barely registered the figure in the doorway. In fact, he would not register anything again. The bullet entered through his forehead, exited the back of his skull and punched a 9mm hole through the thin metal skin of the van.

Flynn's body slumped back into the payload bay as the tools fell from his dead hands; his death a matter of precaution.

Chapter Eighteen

David found himself ripped from a pleasantly sensual yet disturbing dream about Rachel. Seeing her naked must have been a more pleasing experience than he allowed himself to believe, but the dream was gone as he was rudely awoken by a pillow being thrown at his head. His eyes opened to see the grinning face of Tom in the doorway.

"No amount of beauty sleep is gonna help that ugly mug."

"What time is it?" David yawned, barely aware of his surroundings.

"Time to eat, I'm starving." Tom said.

David sat up and grabbed his phone to see what the actual time was. It was a little after five.

"I've been asleep for a few hours. I need a tea before I eat." David smiled at his friend in a knowing way.

"I'm not making you one. We are guests. I'm sure your Mom will make you one." Tom argued.

"She's not my mother." David hated when Tom said that.

"Step Mom?"

"Piss off!" David got up and threw the pillow back at his friend.

After a friendly exchange of banter the pair went downstairs. Rachel was already in the lounge, a steaming mug of coffee on the table in front of her. She wore leggings and a loose fitting low cut white top with no bra.

"Kettle has just boiled. Do you want a drink?" She said getting to her feet.

The pair nodded in agreement and sat on the same sofa as they had done when they first arrived. Tom pushed his tongue into his cheek and shook his head at his friend. Tom did that when he liked how a woman dressed or if she was particularly attractive. David did not want to know what his friend was thinking.

"Do you want to eat now or later? It makes no difference to me but you boys have travelled and stuff. So we can eat now if you like or I can break out some biscuits to keep you going? What do you want to do?"

"Biscuits, please!" Tom never did stand on ceremony but was on his feet pretty quick for the offer of something to dunk in his tea.

David grabbed the back of his jeans and pulled him back down onto the sofa.

"I'll go." David said.

David stood up and walked over to the kitchen area to offer some assistance. There was still the awkwardness between them and he did not want to spoil the funeral, not that a funeral can be spoiled really. He thought that maybe some casual interaction would bridge the gap between them. There was no real indicator of the problem. David thought maybe it was the fact that his father's girlfriend was just a few years younger than he was. Usually a step mother figure would be considerably older or that is how it was.

David leaned over the kitchen counter.

"Can I help?" He said trying to be jovial.

"You can take the biscuits over." She said as she crouched down in front of him. "There's a choice, digestives or ginger biscuits?"

"GINGER BISCUITS!" was shouted from the lounge. Tom had picked up a copy of the local paper and was thumbing through it.

"Ginger biscuits, I think?" David repeated to Rachel with an embarrassing smile upon his face.

She leaned into the cupboard and her top fell forward revealing her breasts to David. He could see a nipple and her tanned flesh all the way down to her pierced navel. He quickly turned away and look toward Tom, who sat reading the paper, oblivious to what was on show.

"Er. What are…you reading?" David stumbled out a question for his friend.

"The really depressing local news," Tom said without raising his eyes from the page, "car crime, burglary, and some story about guy with cancer running away. Did you bring any DVDs? I fancy a film."

Rachel stood up and placed the packet of biscuits on the counter.

"What's the name of the guy in that story? Also, there are some films in the drawer of the coffee table if you want to watch one." She said trying to join in the conversation.

"It says here, Paul Barnard, aged 53 from Clifton." Tom answered.

"He used to work at the site. Got diagnosed with terminal cancer, brain tumour I think, he left a note and disappeared." Rachel looked sad again, "He's got a wife and three daughters."

"Tragic!" Tom uttered in mock empathy.

David took the biscuits into the lounge area. His face felt hot from embarrassment and he sat down next to Tom hoping for some kind of distraction from his friend.

"Alright?" David said wanting some interaction to help calm his blushing.

"Yeah, I can see her nipples through that top," Tom's voice was quiet and his eyes did not move from the newspaper, "and I think she got the hots for you."

David prayed that his friend was just trying to get a rise out of him. He would soon find out, one way or another.

Chapter Nineteen

Jones drove the beaten up old van to a secluded spot in the woods, just a half a mile from the layby. There was an old dirt road than ran up to an old pump house for the industrial estate. As the site was abandoned, so was the pump house. Foliage had grown over the old parking bay that the service engineers would have used. The door and window of the pump house were missing also. No doubt characters, like the one that lay dead in the back of the van, had ransacked the building for all the valuable material years ago.

As he stepped out of the van Jones noticed that he could actually see the near side of the estate from the pump house. He could just make out the Land Rover where he had left the body of Bailey. The silhouette of man with a dog running free could be seen heading in that direction. The slight rise of the hill where the pump house was, made it impossible to see the van from that location, hopefully it would be enough cover to conceal the body dump.

Jones walked around to the side door and opened it. Some of the blood had started to congeal on the wooden floor, not that there was much. There was more splatter over the roof and wall of the van than anywhere else. Still he would have to be careful not to get any on his clothes, as the decorator's coveralls had already been discarded. He reached into the pocket of the dead man and pulled out a mobile phone.

The phone was the reason for this execution. As Jones had driven out of the site after killing Bailey he had seen the blue van approaching from the opposite side of the estate. He observed the van turn and park right outside the disused building where Bailey's car had been left. Being prepared, Jones had pulled out a pair of small binoculars and parked up where he had an uninterrupted view of the van's driver. He could see the man was speaking on a mobile phone to someone. Who, he did not know, but he could not take the chance that he had not been spotted and decided to take the man out. He would check the numbers after he had put some distance between himself and the two crime scenes.

One death or several it was all the same to him. Jones had no way of knowing how many people he had killed during his lifetime. Some were legitimate kills. He had been in the army and seen action in the first Gulf War and Bosnia, but also he had been a soldier for hire after he left the service; mainly working in Africa as close protection or sometimes as security on tankers and freighters that were vulnerable to attack from pirates. Up to that point the number of kills he was responsible for were in single figures. Until a chance meeting in an airport eight years ago he had never considered being what is essentially a hitman.

Jones had been sitting in a departure lounge waiting for a flight out to Oman. He had been hired by a private security company to be part of an armed deployment to protect tankers that negotiated the Gulf of Aden, just off the Somalian coast. A protection crew would be taken by local fishermen out to a vulnerable ship in the Arabian Sea, once on board the four-man team would take it in shifts to guard the ship through the Gulf of Aden and the full length of the Red

Sea. The team would disembark at the Suez Canal and either board another ship requiring protection in the opposite direction or fly back to Oman to repeat the process. The job paid very well and there was little trouble, nothing more than a few shots fired across the bow of a pirate boat. Jones could earn a soldier's annual wage in a month depending on the company he worked for.

As he sipped on a beer while reading a newspaper, somebody came and sat next to him. It was Ryan Mitchell, an old army buddy. The first thing that struck Jones was the guy that he had not seen in a few years, who usually wore jeans or combats with an old T-shirt, was dressed in an expensive suit and looked a world away from the committed squaddie that Jones once knew.

"How are you McNabbs?" Mitchell asked. McNabbs was the nickname that he gave to soldiers that failed S.A.S. selection as Jones had.

"I'm good. You look wealthy. Won the lottery?" He responded.

"Life after the army is better to some than others." Mitchell spoke with a confidence that financial security afforded. This was a very different man than the cash strapped heavy drinker that Jones had known.

"Clearly! I do ok. What are you doing these days?"

"I'm not working the tankers in the middle east, that's for sure." There was smugness in the comment.

"The moneys good and I'm not fussy about what I do." Jones was starting to get annoyed by his old colleague.

"If you do get fussy, you should contact this guy." Mitchell handed him a plain white business card that had nothing but a UK mobile phone number. "You were a good soldier and you could do well at my game."

"What is your game?" He stared at the card looking to see if the missing information would magically appear.

Mitchell did not answer.

"Take care of yourself McNabbs." Mitchell said getting to his feet. "I may catch you again sometime."

Mitchell turned and left.

Jones kept the number safe but still caught the flight.

On his return to the UK six weeks later he decided to give the number a call.

"Yes." The voice at the end of the phone had no discernible accent at all.

"Er...yeah...hello. I was given your number by a friend of mine. My name is..."

"No names, one job, one day, one thousand pounds, yes or no."

"Er...yes!" Jones said.

"Do you drive?"

"Yes."

"Leigh Delamere Services, west bound M4, two days from now at 11pm, park at the far end of the car park and wait for a phone call." The line went dead.

Two days later Jones was sat in the near empty service station carpark. He had arrived early and watched for any signs of life. The occasional car came into the services as did a few HGVs. There were no more than a dozen cars in the car park in total with no visible occupants, although the carpark was quite large and he could not determine what the make and model of the cars were at the opposite end, so spotting people sitting inside was near impossible. Sure enough at 11pm exactly his phone rang.

"To your left there is a black Audi." The same voice as before said.

"I see it." Jones said.

"Leave everything that identifies you in your car, mobile phone, wallet, bank cards, driving license."

"Ok."

"Everything you need will be in the Audi. Do the job well and there will be more work for you. Do it badly and you will never work again. Understood?" The voice said

"Understood!" The statement bothered him, 'Never work again' for the mysterious man or for anybody, ever?

Jones did as he was asked and walked over to the Audi. It was unlocked and the keys were in the ignition. He climbed in but before he could get comfortable and adjust the seat, a phone rang. Jones picked up the mobile from the door pocket and answered it.

"In the boot is a box. Use what is inside. Get in, do it, get out," It was the same voice again. "Use the back entrance." The line went dead.

He got out of the car and opened the boot. There was a cardboard box about a foot square. He removed the lid and inside was a Satnav, a Beretta 9mm handgun and a photograph of a man. Jones got back into the car and mounted the Satnav to the windscreen and switched it on. After a moment a pre-programmed route popped up on the screen. He put the Beretta into the glove compartment and tucked the photo into his shirt pocket. The mobile rang again as he switched on the ignition.

"The Satnav will take you to the place. The weapon is the tool. The man in the picture is the job. Are you clear, yes or no?"

"You want me to.." Jones started to say.

"Use your imagination but do not state the obvious. You have a place, a job and a weapon. Figure it out for yourself and come up with the correct answer." The line went dead.

Jones scrolled through the phones contact list. It was empty. The incoming calls had been withheld. The man said he had a place, a tool and a job, so he followed the instructions giving by the Satnav.

Two hours later the Audi pulled up in a dark alley behind a night club in Hounslow. Booming music could be heard vibrating the walls. The air in the alley was alive with the sound waves.

Jones stepped out of the car, taking the gun with him and tucked it in to his waistband.

The only illumination in dank alley came from dim fire exit lights at the rear of the few buildings that backed onto it. The nightclub was no different. There was a double fire exit door with a dim emergency light above.

Jones approached the door. There was no mistake that this was the correct building. He could see a figure walking toward him from the other end of the alley. The figure was a short, slight man with young features dressed head to toe in matching grey sportswear. Jones walked passed the door and continued until he passed the man. He continued walking slowly but looked over his shoulder to see where the man was going.

Sportswear man walked straight up to the door and knocked firmly on the metal. Jones stopped against the wall and stayed in the shadows. After a minute, the door opened and a face appeared at the gap. The man in sportswear handed what Jones thought must be some money. The face at the door took the money and then handed the man something. The something was placed deep into a pocket and the man rushed off back the way he came, glancing cautiously at Jones as he passed.

Jones remained where he was and stood waiting for the next customer, which was very soon. He could hear the clipping along the pavement in the distance before they entered the alley but merely a few seconds after the sportswear man had disappeared, two young ladies dressed in skimpy short dresses and vertigo inducing heels tottered into view. They laughed and giggled whilst holding on to each other for support, not only because the difficult footwear but also the volume of alcohol each had obviously consumed. It was impossible to be invisible as the women walked passed but Jones did his best and failed. The nearest woman, in a bright pink miniscule dress looked at him and then whispered something to her friend, who laughed out loud from the comment.

Once they had reached the door the laughing woman, in an even smaller blue dress, kicked the door with her towering shoes. Lifting her leg made her dress ride up, affording Jones a view of some very tiny underwear that hardly covered her buttocks.

Again, after a minute the door opened and face appeared in the gap but this time the man stepped out from the dark club doorway and into the dim light to embrace both women.

"How are my girls tonight? You's is looking fine." He said switching on the charm for his customers. This man was also wearing sportswear and had an oversized baseball cap perched on his head.

The girls mumbled and giggled a response but Jones did not hear what was said as the open door had let the pent up heavy bass music escape into the alley.

"Well I is feeling generous tonight. 'Specially as you ladies look so fine." The man kept moving and swaying in front of the women as he looked them both up and down, every now and then he would touch one of the women as they laughed along to whatever he was saying.

The trio talked quietly for a few moments and Jones suddenly recognised the would-be lothario. It was the man in the photograph. He looked different because of the hat but it was definitely the same man. Jones continued to watch as the man kept swaying and the girls kept tottering and giggling.

Once enough small talk had been made, the deal came next. The voices were hushed to keep the transaction a secret, although there were only a few things that took place in a pitch black alley in the early hours of the morning; sex or drugs.

The man reached into his jacket pocket and slipped something into the handbag of the girl in the blue dress. He whispered in her ear and then wrapped his arms around her slim young body. He forcibly kissed the woman, probing his tongue deep into her mouth while his hands dropped down her back to her now exposed buttocks. His hands squeezed the soft round flesh and fingers slipped beneath underwear material. The woman responded for just a moment but then pushed him away.

The same was repeated with the other woman but this time the man squeezed her breasts through her dress and tried to free one from the low cut tight material. The other woman grabbed her friend by the arm and pulled her away from the man. They had what they wanted and it had only cost them a drunken fumble, instead of the money they were more than happy to pay when they kicked the door.

"I'll see you ladies again. If yous is passing later, bang the door and we can party. There's more where that came from..." the man comments fell on deaf ears as the girls clipped away, giggling between themselves and ignoring the man's vain attempts to keep the women interested. "...Laters ladies."

With a disappointed expression on his face, the man stepped back into the club. He slammed the door and the volume of the music dropped once more.

Jones stepped out of the shadows and walked slowly toward the fire exit door. He stopped directly in front of the door and could feel the metal vibrating as it tried to contain the music. With a quick glance in both directions, Jones pulled the gun from his waist band and stood with both hands behind his back. There was a moment of trepidation but he decided to do the job quickly instead of delay anymore. He kicked the door, twice.

The minute delay he was expecting concluded with the door opening just 8 inches to reveal the man's face, the peak of his cap determining the opening as it was wider than the man's head.

"What do you want, granddad?" the man spat.

"To do some business," Jones said with a neutral voice.

"What business?"

"Ya know! Business!" It was all he could say.

"Yo fuck you man." The sportswear wearing drug dealer pushed the door all the way open and stepped into Jones face. "If yous is knocking on my door, then yous knows what business yous is doing."

"I want some stuff." Jones was buying some time. The man was in his face and was probably no more than five feet five tall and seriously skinny. The black void beyond the door had the occasional flashing coloured light but there seemed to be no other bodies hidden in the darkness.

"Yous don't knows what you want granddad, so fuck off out my alley before I kick yo ass for yous." The man exclaimed whilst pointing a finger in the bigger man's face.

Jones backed away and luckily the distance was not closed by more threats from the animated figure. The man raised his hand and pointed a sideways finger at him like a gangsta in a rap video holding an imaginary handgun, his thumb extended before closing against his hand as the imaginary pistol was fired.

The man was not able to re-cock the thumb of his hand. Two bullets in quick succession hammered through the man's chest. The force of the shots pushed him back through the doorway, his feet stayed on the outside while his body fell inside. Jones stepped forward and looked down at the man. He could see the fixed death gaze of the man's open eyes beneath the peak of the cap that refused to leave his head. Jones fired one more bullet into the man's head. Then he turned and ran back towards the borrowed car. For his first job, that seemed incredibly easy.

Chapter Twenty

As the dented and rusting white van entered the Severn Gate site, Jimmy spotted the corner of a police car. The vehicle was mostly hidden by the tall over grown foliage of an industrial site that had fallen into disorder. He stopped the van and got out, but left the keys in the ignition and the engine running.

"Stay here." He said to Billy who pensively sat in the passenger seat.

Jimmy ran toward the nearest building. He moved quickly for a heavy set man and not a lumbering oaf like Billy was. He pressed his body flat to the wall and peered around the corner. He could see two police cars and an ambulance parked in front of one of the more intact structures on the site. The back of the ambulance was open and a police officer was talking to a dog walker. All the other service personnel had their attention focused on the shed attached to the building. Jimmy cursed as he was not able to see the inside of the shed from where he was. He could just hear conversation but was too far away to make out what was being said. A policeman came out of the shed and had a large clear plastic envelope in his hand. Jimmy could not be sure but the enveloped looked like it contained a magazine of some kind.

There was no way that Jimmy could manoeuvre his way into getting a better view without being seen or having to do a complete circuit of the perimeter. He made his way back to the van.

"What did you see Jimmy?" Billy asked with anticipation.

"Not enough." He rammed the van into reverse and span around swiftly.

"What next?"

"We're going to see the Pikey." Jimmy said with an amazing amount of control in his voice. Normally he would have just silenced his brother's questions but he needed Billy to know what was happening. If something happened to him he would need his young brother in his corner. Visiting Pete 'The Pikey' Flynn was often problematic. The Pikey was one of the few men Jimmy was actually scared of. But it was Flynn that had phoned Jimmy with the information about the discovery of Bailey's car.

Jimmy guessed that Flynn had probably been down on the site looking for scrap metal. The abandoned buildings were a great place for joyriders to dump stolen cars and Flynn liked to get to them before the law did. Not that Flynn was bothered by the law. The only law he recognised was the traditions of the travelling community and he fought hard for those values with his pride and his fists. Flynn was also a fourth generation bare knuckle boxing champion. Jimmy and Flynn had come to blows on occasion. The two men respected but did not trust each other. The old gangster adage 'Keep your friends close but keep your enemies closer' was why they kept in touch. They were too close sometimes.

Chapter Twenty One

Like many members of the travelling community, Flynn had put down roots and bought a house, married a local girl and had a few kids. The wife and kids had long since left but the latest girlfriend would be home if The Pikey was not.

The Kinsellas pulled up in their battered van. Jimmy got out but told Billy to stay put. He knew that Billy annoyed Flynn with his constant questions. Even though he suspected Flynn probably was not at home, as his van was gone, he did not want Flynn to arrive back home and be frustrated by the younger brothers constant rambling.

Jimmy banged on the front door. He could hear some activity from inside the house before he could see a figure approach the frosted glass of the front door. It opened about a foot and Sarah, Flynn's current girlfriend stuck he head through the gap.

"What do ya want?" Her voice was harsh and rapid. She was of the travelling community too, a very pretty woman in her day and a decade or more, younger than Flynn, but the years of drinking and smoking had aged her terribly and she had an aggressive personality which made her instantly less attractive.

"Where's Flynn?" Jimmy was not intimidated by her abrasive nature in fact he quite liked it. He quite liked her at least he did, a few years ago.

"I don't fuckin' know. Fuck off Jimmy I've just got out of the shower."

Jimmy pushed the door open more than Sarah had allowed. He could see that she was in a short dressing gown. The belt was not tied tight and he could see some cleavage plus it was too short to go beyond her knees and exposed her shapely calves.

"Don't you look nice?" He said with a leery smile, "When will he be back? He's not answering his phone."

"Fuck off, Jimmy." They had history and she was not sure what he might do. "I don't know when he'll be back. It could be any minute."

She tried to close the door on him but Jimmy had put his foot inside to prevent her from closing it anymore.

Jimmy looked towards his brother who was watching from the van. He gave his younger sibling the lookout signal by pointing two fingers in a 'V' towards his own eyes and then pointing the fingers out to the street, then raised a thumb to see if Billy understood. He did.

Jimmy stepped into the house uninvited.

"Jimmy! Get the fuck out of the house man!" Sarah protested but she liked that Jimmy still wanted her after all these years. Before she was with Flynn, about twelve years previously, she and Jimmy used to drink at the same pubs. There was always flirting, laughing and teasing throughout an evening of heavy drinking. One time, the flirting escalated to a drunken fumble in the carpark. That evolved into regular drunken sex, either against a wall or on a park bench or wherever was convenient but never in the comfort of a bed. It was animalistic, aggressive sex fuelled by too much booze and false confidence. Eventually, the regular cycle was broken by Jimmy having to do a stretch for GBH. Once he was released Sarah was already with Flynn. She liked rough aggressive men to dominate her, which they often did. Flynn was a harder man in all respects and worked harder than Jimmy ever could. Although not completely honest, Flynn was not a criminal. Jimmy was a criminal with plenty of form, and he only worked when he needed to lay low. He wanted to lay low now; with Flynn's woman.

Jimmy stood pinning her into the corner of the hall. His hands pulled at her dressing gown.

"No, no, no, Jimmy." She said 'No' but there was a lack of conviction in her voice.

Her gown fell open revealing her naked, damp body. The flowery scent of shower gel escaped along with her dignity and self-control.

"Mmmm, I've missed you Sarah." Jimmy gazed down at her breasts, which were not as big as he remembered, and shaved area of her pubis, which was the norm these days but not when they used to share their sexual experiences in the dark, nocturnal corners of the city.

"Stop it, Jimmy. Pete will be back soon." She half-heartedly pulled her gown across her body but only managed to cover her breasts.

Jimmy reached down between her legs and gently stroked the smooth stubble free mound that was still exposed. A hand gripped his wrist to stop him but there was little resistance, merely a gesture of protest. He spread his fingers over the area, slowly using his first and third finger he parted the soft flesh and carefully pushed his middle finger into her. Her eyes closed and she gasped, the grip on his wrist increased but this time it was not to push his attentions away. He slowly slid his finger in and out while cupping her most intimate area. The years seemed to roll back as he leaned forward and kissed her hard on the lips. She responded and placed her hands on the back of his head as if to pull his tongue deeper into her mouth. He felt her push her hips toward him rhythmically, matching the ever increasing stroking of his finger inside her.

The house phone rang and shocked the pair back into the present and the reality of what they were doing.

"Get out now Jimmy. You've had your fun." This time she could fully cover her body with the gown and pushed him away. She reached for the door and opened it.

"Not as much as I'd have liked." He laughed at her and put his middle finger against his tongue, "You still taste the same. You taste good." He turned and walked out of the door with a smug grin across his face.

She slammed the door behind him and felt angry at herself for giving into the same old rough charm. She was aroused. She liked the attention but it was Jimmy's will to touch her and not her desire to be touched, as sensual and pleasing as it was.

She picked up the phone.

"Hello…" That was the only thing she said. The information she received chilled her into silence. Flynn had been found.

Chapter Twenty Two

The sunlight poured through the gap in the badly drawn curtains and shone directly on to David's face. His sleep had been fitful and disturbed but now he was fully awake, rolling over to shield his eyes before deciding whether now was a good time to get out of bed or not.

The previous night had not been as bad as he thought it might be. He and Tom had popped round to the local Chinese takeaway and ordered several different meals to share plus all the usual prawn crackers, chips, noodles and rice. Tom had insisted they buy enough food for at least four people but Rachel had had some rice and a couple of chicken balls but very little else. Subsequently, David and Tom tried to put a huge dent in the food order but ended up bloated and uncomfortable.

Rachel had taken herself off to bed while the friends watched a couple of movies. Tom wanted to watch the Bourne Identity as it was the only film in the flat that he knew he would enjoy. David preferred Schindler's List. As they had the time, they watched both. Although, Tom kept uttering 'I will find you and will kill you' the memorable line from the movie Taken every time Liam Neeson appeared on screen.

They had gone to their beds just after midnight but David could not sleep properly because of the weight of stodgy food in his gut and the thought of the funeral. That had made the sun's intrusion very unwelcome after such a heavy night.

He threw on a pair of joggers and a t-shirt and tip toed barefoot downstairs, the feel of the naked wooden steps felt rough under foot. No sooner had he filled the kettle and flicked it on, Rachel silently padded into the room.

"Morning!" She said, half yawning.

"Morning, do you want a drink?" David asked even though he was the house guest.

"Thank you, coffee, black, one sweetener please." She then stretched her arms and shuffled over to the dining table and lifted some coasters out of the drawer, dropping them randomly across the wooden surface.

He watched her as she opened to the curtains to let in more of the sun's awakening brightness. The light shone through the thin white, knee-length nightshirt she was wearing to reveal her slim waist and hips which flared out to match her dancer's thighs that tapered in at the knees, her tiny ankles and athletic calves were on show the whole time. When she turned around and walked back toward the kitchen, David noticed that he could see through the material without the sun's help. It was obvious that she had no underwear beneath the nightshirt. He looked away and felt slightly ashamed that he was aroused by her.

"Did you sleep ok?" He asked trying to look at her face and at no other part of her body.

"So, so. You?"

"The same,"

The kettle clicked off and David poured the water into the mugs. In the silence that followed he could hear the faint snoring of Tom coming from the spare room. Rachel knew what David was thinking.

"It's a good job you didn't have to share." She smiled but not a sincere smile.

"Yeah." He answered just for something to say. He longed for the day to be over so that he and Tom could get their heads down and leave the following morning. The sooner they were out of the city and back in Wales, the better he would feel.

"We are being picked up at ten coz the church is so far away" she said to break the silence again.

"Ok. Then on to a hotel you said, for the wake?"

"That's right. I'm gonna need a drink before we go." She reached into the fridge and pulled out a half drank bottle of white wine and poured it into a tumbler.

David checked the clock. It was 6.47am. It was going to be a very long day indeed.

Chapter Twenty Three

Jimmy sat at the kitchen table and stubbed out yet another cigarette into the overflowing ashtray that was empty when he first sat down. He had received a call from Ducty just before midnight, who had told him about Flynn being found dead in the back of his dumped van. Ducty had not been certain and his source was not to be completely trusted but the word on the street was that Flynn had been executed. A single gunshot wound to the head was automatically deemed to be the work of a hitman, whether it was true or not.

Billy had gone to bed as soon as they returned to their flat. Jimmy always stayed up after his brother and rose before him too but he had not slept at all this night. He just stayed perched at the table with two packets of cigarettes, a lighter and the local rag; a cigarette almost accompanied every page. He read every article completely before moving on to the next and recognised name after name in many of the stories. The two that he was most familiar with were John Hill and Paul Barnard; one dead, one missing. Jimmy had worked with both. And although Hill had sacked him and his brother a few weeks ago, he bore the man no ill will. Hill had the respect of the entire criminal under class. He was an important man and well respected.

Night turned into morning slowly and brought a kind of foreboding the Jimmy was unfamiliar with.

He had spent time in prison, been a wanted man and constantly looked over his shoulder for past wrongdoings returning to seek vengeance on him, but this was different. As a career criminal he had developed a paranoia that had kept him and his brother safe for many years, but this was an extreme feeling of fear. He knew that Duncs must have been killed. And now the man that had called Jimmy about it, was also dead. If there was some kind of link between the deaths then a professional killer would know who Flynn had called and why. Jimmy could have been overthinking the whole situation but overthinking had proved to be effective in the past and kept him one step ahead.

He sparked up another cigarette and stepped over to the kettle to put it on. He had to try and find out as much as possible but for now it would have to be put on hold. The day may present some answers without too much effort but he would have to wait and see. Also Billy would be up soon and they had a funeral to go to, even though they would not be welcome.

Chapter Twenty Four

Jones had woken early and completed his morning routine of exercise and evidence removal. He had already heard about the discovery of Flynn's body. Until that point he did not have a name for the man but once the information had come his way, he realised that he knew of the man and his reputation.

Taking care of a problem is always an 'act now, think later' situation but practice makes perfect. He did not need Flynn to be hidden for a long time, just long enough. The disposal of the van and the body did mean that Jones was unable to move Bailey's car to a more suitable location before it was discovered and the police were called.

The decision to kill Flynn may come back to haunt him, but it was the right thing to do under the circumstances. He could not take the risk that Flynn had seen him and reported it to someone that could get to him. The only concern was that Flynn was a big noise amongst the other travellers; a bare knuckle fighter of some repute and all the local travellers in his corner. Gypsies, Pikeys or travellers by any other name, they were fiercely loyal to their own kind, following their own traditions and laws.

Jones was loyal to the highest bidder for his kind of work. He was known among the upper echelons of the criminal class across the Midlands, South of England and within certain select groups across Europe. He only killed when it was a necessity of the job and if the pay was suitable. A clan of travellers worked for less and had more to lose from failure.

Jones hoped that his snap reaction to take out a potential witness would not be a mistake.

The dead man's mobile phone was charging on the dressing table of the budget hotel and it was the only thing that Jones had taken from the body, so it was the only thing that could place him at the scene. The last number dialled was a mobile number under the name of 'Jimmy K', the call duration was only 27 seconds long. Jones doubted that much information could be exchanged in such a short call but it would depend on what was said. The call could have been just a message left on an answerphone which, to some degree, was worse as the information would stay on the message until deleted and could be easily recorded.

He scrolled through the contents of the phone logs and the most called numbers were to 'Sarah' and 'Ducty', Jones knew of Ducty. Everybody with any link to criminal gangs that dealt in drugs was familiar with the name. Ducty was a middle man for the local small scale dealers. Jones knew that he would have to pay him a visit. Like himself, Ducty worked for more than one criminal fraternity and was an important part of the distribution network. Jones would have to be careful not to bite the hand that feeds him. If Ducty was under the pay of the same gangs as Jones was then he might reduce his work opportunities, plus anger some powerful people; people that could afford others in the same line of work as Jones and use them to 'adjust' his mistake, if Ducty came to any harm. Interrogate but not kill was the line he would have to follow. He only needed to know who 'Jimmy K' was and how much of a threat he could be.

Chapter Twenty Five

David had showered and was now dressed in his black suit, white shirt and black tie. The black shoes that he had bought just three days previously were pinching already. Refusing the advice to break them in early may have been a mistake that he would pay for all day.

Tom was also ready and looked more the part as he wore a black shirt with his black suit and tie. David had joked that he looked more like a reject from a crap boyband but Tom did not rise to the banter as it was he who set the banter.

The pair paced the lounge area waiting for the car to arrive. It would not be coming for another fifteen minutes but they were still impatient to go. Not because they were looking forward to the funeral, but because they needed to change the scenery. Less than twenty-four hours in the city and the awkward atmosphere was already wearing them both down.

Rachel clipped in on over knee-high boots with spike heels. The little black dress she wore was tight around her slim shapely figure. Just a few inches of black stocking were visible between the top of the boots and the hem of her dress. The outfit was striking, more for a glamourous night out than a funeral. She would turn some heads today, but then she did anyway. It was often her goal.

There were a few moments of nervous silence as the trio stood uncomfortably waiting. The minutes counted down too slowly but eventually there was the parping of a car horn from the street to which Rachel reacted. She glanced out of the window and then just nodded at the pair. They let Rachel lead the way and followed her outside.

The day was cool and breezy even though it was sunny and cloudless. David descended the steps behind Rachel. He found it difficult not to watch her walk; even that was attractive. He hoped the car was big enough that he did not need to sit next to her. Physical contact along with physical attraction was not a combination he wanted to mix.

The car was a stretched BMW, it had six doors. Two rear doors meant two rows of seats. David instinctively got into a different row than Rachel so he would not be sitting next to her but he soon realised this was an error. The seating in the back of the car had the seats facing each other, so he now sat face to face with Rachel.

Already in the car was a man that David recognised but was not sure where from. Also an older lady, the man's wife he presumed, and a younger woman who could be their daughter, as she was very similar to the older lady.

"This is Phil Dobbs, your father's right hand man." Rachel introduced.

The two men shook hands then Tom also offered his hand.

"This is my wife Lorna and our daughter Molly." Dobbs said in a strong Irish accent. David and Tom again offered their hands and their names to be polite.

Dobbs was sitting between his daughter and Rachel so it was easy for him to converse with David and Tom. Dobbs did most of the talking on the way to the service.

"You're like your father. Same eyes, same nose. Like two peas you are." Dobbs said.

"Thank you." David did not know what else to say.

"I worked with your dad for almost forty years, and we've run the company together for nearly twenty five years, since before Molly was born," He looked and smiled at his daughter, "And now she works for the firm too."

"What do you do?" David asked her directly hoping to encourage her father to be quiet.

"She's a receptionist in the site office with Rachel." Dobbs answered the question.

"Cool!" was all David could offer.

In fact the whole thirty minute journey involved Dobbs talking about the business and John Hill. How they had landed the Diamond project which was worth millions to the firm and there were more big contracts lined up. How there were electricians, plumbers, carpenters, brickies and surveyors, all on the payroll. The list of information went on and on. David took to giving three different responses to all statements; 'Yeah!', 'Great!' and 'Really!'

All the time that Dobbs talked, David could only give him eye contact for a moment. He could not help but look at the man's daughter. Molly was stunning. Not beautiful in the conventional sense but beautiful in the very real sense of the word. She was tall and slim with pale skin and bright blonde hair. Her face was elfin like. Huge blue eyes set above high cheekbones that tapered down to her cheeks which were flawless. She had full pouting lips which were covered in bright red lipstick but very little other makeup. She looked like she should be a model. David had never seen a face so captivating. As soon as he had set eyes on Molly all thoughts of his inappropriate attraction toward Rachel had vanished.

As they neared the church Rachel spoke for the first time since the introduction of Dobbs.

"We'll take the car to the wake and then have to get a taxi back. Is that ok for you boys?"

"Yes that's fine." David said and noticed Rachel staring at him. He held her gaze for a moment then smiled and dropped his head wishing he had not looked at all. Rachel had deliberately pointed her knees toward him and parted them slightly, exposing the tops to her stockings and her lacy panties. He raised his eyes to look at her to see if she had seen where his eyes just were but Rachel had turned her head to look out of the window. He could feel the heat in his face and hoped nobody could see his blush.

They were all glad to get out of the warm car and into the cool spring air. Rachel automatically linked arms with him as they were supposed to be there for each other's support and linked her other arm with Tom. They never looked at her as they walked along the long path that led into the large gothic church, centred in a small village on the outskirts of the city.

There were a significant number of people at the church waiting to go in, many smoking and chatting but others were grim faced and silent. David assumed that they had to be work colleagues and friends as there were so many. As they passed, some of the faces gazed respectfully at the chief mourners, others were wondering who they were.

Hidden toward the back of the crowd were the Kinsella brothers. Dressed in their Sunday best and smoking heavily, trying to remain unnoticed by Rachel, or anyone who thought they should not be there.

What nobody could see was the man watching from a black BMW; parked on the road on the opposite side of the graveyard. Jones lowered his binoculars and wondered which man was the grieving son. He was sure he would know by the end of the day.

Chapter Twenty Six

The service had been a very tasteful affair. No readings, a couple of hymns and a song by The Moody Blues. With the burial, the whole event was over in ninety minutes. David had estimated the church held about two hundred people and there was standing room only. He did not know the social circles his father was drawn to, but David thought he could have been at a gangster's funeral. Every man there looked as if he had done 'time' at some stage in his life. There were only a couple of dozen women, most had to be the wives of the rough looking men that attended.

If David was honest with himself, he was only looking at one person throughout the service and at the graveside. He was drawn to Molly. As with most straight men, David liked to look at an attractive woman and enjoyed their company but he found it difficult to commit to a relationship. But he found the fears that confined him to a single life had melted away upon every word with a soft Irish inflection that fell from her lips.

With the service over with there was just the wake to get through. David hoped that he might be able to spend some time talking to Molly without Tom spoiling the conversation with his constant jokes and sarcastic comments. As good a friend as he was, he could be irritating at all the wrong moments.

The wake was being held in a nearby hotel, a large manor house with expansive grounds called The Royal Oaks Hotel. It was the type of place that could cater for a wedding and a funeral on the same day but neither of the parties would meet because of the vastness of the location.

Before his death, John Hill had stated that he would like his funeral party to be held at The Oaks, as it was known locally, and Rachel had said that it would be booked if anything ever happened to him. She was true to her word.

The mourners were led through to a large function room with a bar toward the back of the hotel. There was a large buffet table filled with the usual fayre. Sandwiches, sausage rolls, pasta, and various types of dessert items were spread the full length of the table. There were also a few bottles of wine and some glasses on a separate table.

Not everyone from the church came to the hotel but David was glad that Molly had. He watched Phil hobble in with his wife of his arm. David had not noticed before but the old man had a very pronounced limp but maybe it was from an injury on site or something like that. David was just presuming.

Tom came over and thrust a pint of lager into David's hand.

"You look like you need that fella." Tom was not wrong.

David lifted the glass to his lips and downed a third of the liquid in one gulp. He gave an audible gasp as an exclamation of relief.

"I do, but not too many."

"Have you seen Rachel?" Tom asked.

"No, she must be in the ladies." David craned his neck to try and find her but he stopped looking when he saw Molly making her way toward him through the crowd.

"No, she's at the wine table pouring her second glass fella." Tom had seen her drain a glass within minutes of them entering the room.

"Jesus! I hope she holds it together." He got the statement out before Molly could hear it.

Molly arrived with a cheeky, wide smile. Her eyes were a deep blue like a tropical lagoon on some far away Pacific Isle. That is where he had been wishing he was, far away, until Molly walked right up to him. Their eyes locked and the pause seemed like an eternity, he rummaged through his brain for something to say but she beat him too it.

"Tough day at the office?" she posed the ambiguous question.

"Excuse me?" He was unprepared to answer as the daydream he was caught in had emptied his mind.

"You look a little overwhelmed." She clarified what she had intended to say.

"Yeah, definitely. This is my first funeral."

"Bless you," she gripped his hand as a measure of support, "don't worry I'll look after you, unless your friend here has the job."

"It's yours. He only tries to embarrass me." He smiled at her as they both glanced at Tom who was oblivious to their conversation and too busy watching Rachel refilling her glass for a second time.

"She is putting it away over there." Tom said, he looked surprised to see Molly standing there and even more taken aback to see that she was holding David's hand.

David could now see Rachel swigging down a glass of white wine on the other side of the room. It was awkward enough being in her company sometimes but to have her drunk as well made him feel uneasy.

"I'm going to have to deal with her aren't I?" David posed the question hoping for adequate solutions.

"Let me." Molly said as she beckoned over her mother from the bar. Lorna was the mould from which Molly was cast, tall, slim, blonde and with the same bottomless eyes. She was an attractive older woman, in her fifties but she could pass for a decade younger. Molly whispered into her ear and pointed toward Rachel. Lorna simply nodded and made her way over to the wine table.

"There you go. My mother will try and keep her out of trouble." Molly said winking at him.

"Can you sort all my problems like that?" David asked.

"We'll have to see." She laughed and placed her other hand on his arm, stroking it in a display of further support.

After the buffet had been dismantled by the reams of builders and tradesmen that made up the bulk of the remaining funeral party, people started to casually disappear. Within an hour and half of entering the building the party had dropped to half the numbers. There were still groups that seemed they would be there for hours to come and the funeral was a perfect excuse for them to have a day off and get drunk.

David sat talking to Molly about everything and anything; music, movies, television, comedians. They seemed to have quite a lot in common. There was a definite attraction for both of them. The sombre venue or the reason for today's event did not stifle their conversation one bit. David felt something awaken inside. He could not be sure what he felt but when he spoke with Molly, he felt happy; he felt confident.

Tom on the other hand was stuck talking to Phil Dobbs, and by talking, it was more of a listening experience for Tom, although he did get the occasional question in.

"Who are those two guys sitting on their own?" Tom asked nodding toward a table in the far corner.

Phil glanced over his shoulder and his whole demeanour changed. The loud cheery voice he had been conversing with suddenly changed to a hushed tone.

"They're the Kinsellas. Jimmy and Billy, Jimmy is the big one and Billy is the dumb one."

"They don't look very friendly." Tom said.

"Look aren't deceiving , they are an evil pair of bastards." Phil muttered.

"What's their problem? And why are they here?"

"Their problems are too many to list but they used to work for Jay, so they are just paying their respects but probably trying to find out a thing or two."

"Who's Jay?" Asked Tom

"John, your friend's father."

Tom looked across at the brooding brothers for too long. Jimmy caught him looking, put down his drink and stared back.

"Are they dangerous?" Tom said averting his eyes.

"I walk with a limp cos of Jimmy. The fuckin' bastard broke into my old gaffer's house and then broke my knee. I've never been the same since. I used to do a bit of driving, stock car and track days, stuff like that but not after that bastard bent my leg the wrong way." Phil rubbed his knee as if talking about the past made the pain return. "Jay had to give them a job until they fucked up and he sacked them. I was glad to see the back of them so I was." The Irish man gave a little smile announcing that fact.

Tom nudged David who sat next to him.

"Can we get out of her soon?"

"What's the rush?" David asked. He was too busy talking to Molly to want to leave just yet.

"I think I've pissed off the locals." Tom said nodding as secretly as possible towards the brothers.

Molly glanced over and interrupted.

"That's the Kinsellas. If you've pissed them off you'd better leave now." She said with a look of real concern in her face.

"Who are they?" David asked as he was not listening to Phil's ramblings.

"They're called the Cousin Brothers and they are a whole heap of trouble. They worked on the site for a few months and gave me and Rachel the creeps." Molly answered.

"Are they cousins or are they brothers?" Tom asked.

"Both!" Molly explained, "Their mothers are sisters and they have the same dad. The dad, James Kinsella, who the big one is named after, was found beaten to death out by the docks a few years ago. The rumour is Jimmy did it but he's never admitted it."

"Jesus!" David said, "And my dad gave them a job?"

Molly just nodded her head. David could see that she was choosing her words carefully.

"I know from what MY father told me, that the brothers were dangerous teenagers but your dad and one of his…." She laboured over the right word, "..associates, took them in and helped them out. Gave them money, sorted them out with jobs, found them a place to live. They were well looked after but now they have no one, just each other."

"What about the other.." David used her word, "associate? Is he still in the picture?"

"Not anymore. He was found dead of a heart attack in his car earlier this week."

"Jesus! It's like a Greek tragedy around here." David was not wrong.

"Duncan Bailey was his name. He wasn't a nice man. Sleazy. He was always sniffing around Rachel." There was a look of disgust in her eyes as she cast a glance across the room.

"What did my father say about that?"

"They had a big falling out but not about that. I'm not sure what. I know Rachel liked the attention from Bailey. Your father was too good for her."

David said nothing as he was inclined to agree with Molly.

"Why did they get sacked?" Tom interjected with the information that Phil had given him, bringing the Kinsellas back to the conversation.

"They were stealing materials and equipment off the site amongst other things. Jay caught them and sacked them. He didn't want to do it but he had to." Molly's face changed, she had a shade of concern about her now.

"Well let's get out of here then and get Rachel home." David said. It had not escaped his attention that his father's mourning girlfriend had still been able to acquire some wine and was looking worse for wear.

"Do you want me to carry her out for you? I can see that you have bigger fish to fry." Tom asked and gave a knowing wink.

"Oh god please yes." David said. He found it uncomfortable for all the wrong reasons to be physically close to Rachel but the thought of having to hold her up whilst drunk, was not an idea he relished. His concerns were all aimed toward Molly now.

Chapter Twenty Seven

Jones sat patiently. He had parked up at the far side of the car park but with a good view of the entrance of the hotel. He needed to know which of the men that had walked out of the church, was the son of John Hill. Had there been only one new face then it would have been easy but having two men of similar ages walk her into church was problematic.

Jones would need to talk to the son only. He needed to find the shotgun. So far three men were dead and he still had no answers. It was unknown why he needed to find such a random item but he was employed to find it and find it he would.

There was some activity from the front of the hotel. He raised his binoculars and took in what he could see. John Hill's partner Rachel was being helped out to a taxi by one of the men that had accompanied her in and out of the church. Could this be Hill's son? Maybe.

Any answers would not be found here. He would need to follow the taxi back and see what happened back at the flat.

Luckily Jones knew where the flat was. He had staked out the property trying to catch Hill previously but to no avail. There was never a sign of the man who was to be his target. He had to lure Hill out. A false break in to the site had been a perfect rouse to get Hill on site alone. Jones had posed as a police officer and said that there had been some activity on the roof. After Hill responded and turned up. Both the men had gone up to the top of the building to investigate but Jones knew that once they arrived there, only one of them would return the way they came. It was easy to get into Hill's confidence as the two men had never met before. Why would Hill not believe that the man was the police?

Once on the roof, Jones asked the question with a gun in his hand. Where was the shotgun? Hill said that it had been stolen and that it was common knowledge. The story did not change when Hill was standing at the edge looking down; down at the dirty plant yard below where his body was later to be found.

The information that Jones had received was, find the item and bring it back. Eliminate all that knew about it and do not fail to retrieve the item. Success would be highly rewarding, failure was not an option. In Jones' terminology 'failure was not an option' meant that if he did not complete the task, he would be 'removed' and another of his kind would replace him. Jones had no intention of being removed and would deliver on the job at all costs.

He had continued to research the shotgun and it was not a rare item or extremely valuable in any way, shape or form. In his experience, for an item to be in such demand, either it was a vital piece of evidence or it had some value to an individual higher up the food chain of the criminal community.

Jones did not care. He knew he was being paid to complete the job and that was all he cared to about.

Chapter Twenty Eight

The journey back to the flat was one of the most uncomfortable experiences of David's life. They all bundled into the back of a seven seater taxi but Rachel dominated the trip, she was very drunk and very upset. Although she was sat next to Tom, the only person she talked to was Lorna. David and Molly sat at the back but trying to have some conversation was almost impossible. Rachel talked too loudly and kept bursting into tears, then apologised loudly about bursting into tears. This was the cycle until they arrived back at the four storey house in the centre of the city.

Tom helped Rachel up the stairs and took her to her bedroom. Lorna and Molly followed behind and put her to bed.

David stayed downstairs with Phil and put the kettle on. He tried to engage the Irishman in some light hearted banter but Phil was not in the mood.

Phil had lost his friend and partner in business so he was entitled to be upset but there was another element to this that he was not letting on.

"So how long did you say you've known my dad?" David asked in an attempt to now drag information from the man who several hours earlier would not shut up.

"Nearly forty years or so."

"That's a long time to be friends. You must be devastated." David was subtly trying to open him up.

"I've lost a lot of friends over the years." The words were a statement with no intention of explanation.

"I bet." David said no more for now.

Tom walked into the room and could see the relief on his friend's face.

"Man, she is wasted."

"I hope she sleeps it off." David offered.

The three men stood in near silence for a few minutes. The awkwardness was obvious. Between the service and arriving back at the flat, something had spooked Phil. David knew it and Phil knew he knew it.

"Who were those two guys at the funeral, again Phil?" Tom tried to spark up some conversation.

"They are a pair of evil bastards. You don't want to know any more about them so don't ask." Phil's tone was harsh and not at all jovial as it had been.

With that Molly and Lorna could be heard clipping down the stairs. Their arrival was welcome as the atmosphere had become oppressive. Phil could not keep still and his agitation had become all too apparent. Lorna's face changed as she entered the room. She could see that something was up.

"Well boys, we have to be going. Leave her sleep and I'm sure she will ok after a few hours." Lorna instructed as she grabbed Phil by the arm and dragged him out.

"I'm gonna stay a while, just in case Rachel wakes up." Molly piped up but nobody was listening. All eyes were on Phil and Lorna's hasty retreat.

David walked over to the window and looked down at the couple as they made their way along the road. The exchange looked heated but not angry, scared maybe, terrified possibly but definitely not angry. As Lorna dashed around the corner of the road and out of view, Phil could be seen limping as fast as he could behind her but reaching for his phone at the same time. He looked like a very frightened man and then he too was out of sight.

David stood at the window and took in the view of the street below. There were no other people strolling on the pavement. The street seemed very quiet, eerily quiet. The weather had been good all day and there was still warmth to the air outside, yet there was nobody about.

He gazed across the roof tops of the houses at the lower end of the street and stared toward the city centre as if the answers to his many questions would float into view, lifted on the heat that was now escaping as the day was slowly drifting into evening.

Below, in the street a car engine fired up. David watched as the vehicle pulled away. No one had gotten into the vehicle while he was watching. The driver had to have been there all along. He watched as the black BMW rounded the bend and disappeared. Nothing about today seemed to be right but then nothing about this whole trip seemed right at all.

Chapter Twenty Nine

Jimmy drew in as much smoke as his lungs could take and then watched with some satisfaction as he filled the room upon exhaling. He sat at the kitchen table in the small flat, still dressed in the black suit that only made an appearance for funerals. And it would seem that he would be going to a few more funerals in the coming weeks. Pete 'The Pikey' Flynn would have a funeral that the Kinsellas would attend. Not just out of respect but also to show support to the Flynn family which may secure a favour or two in the future. Also, Jimmy wanted to go to see if he could start things up again with Sarah. Some regular action would be preferable than the fortnightly spin around the red light district, which Jimmy used to do with Bailey.

The other funeral he would be attending would be Bailey's. Jimmy missed him at the funeral. The brothers would have shared a ride with him as they usually did to such events. Bailey would have driven his 4x4 and the Kinsellas would have looked like bodyguards, flanking him at all times.

Jimmy had noticed that Bailey seemed to be spending more and more time in their company. He would call them in the morning and invite the brothers over for breakfast and then try and plan out the day for the three of them. Jimmy knew it was not loneliness driving their mentor and role model to always have them around. It felt more like fear.

The mobile started vibrating across the surface of table. Jimmy glanced at the screen before answering to see if the call was worth taking. It was Ducty.

"Yeah!"

"Some info has come my way." Ducty said.

"Spill it!"

"Flynn, Duncs and Jay were all pro hits."

The blood rushed into Jimmy's face. He knew something was wrong with how Bailey had died and it was even more bizarre how Flynn had called it in and was then killed just an hour or so afterwards, but Jay, who would want to kill Jay? Bailey was jealous of his position in the Old Firm but surely that was not enough to warrant a hit. Not these days. It might move Bailey up the ranks and back into the fold with the top guys but then maybe not, as he was not popular.

"How do you know?" Jimmy tried to keep from exploding down the phone.

"I just know. Watch your backs. Bailey was after something."

The line went dead.

The Old Firm; He had not heard it called that for years. There was no old firm so to speak of. All the illegal activities had been replaced with legitimate careers over the years. There were no big criminal jobs anymore or non that Jimmy knew about. Everyone in 'The Old Firm' had taken their chances, made their money and had since moved onto bigger and better things.

Bailey had put most of his ill-gotten gains into his store and carved out a decent living from it. He had that air of loveable rogue meets one-time gangster. For the most part Bailey was not a bad bloke, not in Jimmy's eyes anyway. So why would anyone want to kill him? Maybe it was something from the past, something that Jimmy did not know about? But Bailey did not have the vicious side to him like other would-be criminals had. He used to be a family man until such time as the family grew up and flew the nest and his wife decided to get out while she still had her looks to attract other men. Whatever activity Bailey had been involved in recently, criminal or otherwise, he only played the minor role. In fact, there was very rarely a role for him to play at all.

Jimmy wondered whether Bailey had finally came to the end of his useful life and someone somewhere had decided he needed to be put down like an old farm dog that could not run anymore. This was the worry, as Jimmy worked almost exclusively for Bailey, why would the brothers be needed anymore.

Jimmy decided he would call on Ducty to see what he would have in the way of information and why he was telling him to 'watch his back'? Jimmy had never had to watch his back before and he had no intention to start now.

Chapter Thirty

The evening was very pleasant, even if it was just several hours after his father's funeral, David had enjoyed the company. The ever present best friend in the shape of Tom and the very new but very welcome friend that was Molly, did all they could to take David's mind off his troubles. They had been more than successful.

The trio sat and drank for a few hours while chatting about life, the universe and everything in between. It was the first time that David had spent time in the flat and felt comfortable. He was not sure whether it was because Rachel was sleeping off the wine and was out of the picture or because he had the attention of this beautiful young woman.

Molly decided that she should go as she had work in the morning, even though the site was still in shutdown pending a Health and Safety visit. But David had convinced her to take some time off and come down to visit Pembrokeshire. He sold her beautiful beaches and the breath taking scenery so well he joked about changing his career to one with the local tourist board.

"Ok, ok. I'll come and visit." She giggled as she talked like an excited child at the fairground and when she smiled wide enough to show her perfect white teeth, dimples formed in her cheeks.

"Good, you'll love it. I have a spare room and we can eat out in the evenings." David felt alive for once. Who knew that the funeral of his estranged father would bring this incredible woman into his life, if bad things happen for a reason, then maybe Molly was the reason. David very much hoped so.

"Right I'm gonna call a taxi and get myself home. I'll come here tomorrow and you can travel down with me. I won't know the way otherwise."

"Ok, sounds like a plan but it's easy. You just head towards the sunset and if you drive in to the sea, you've gone too far." David had never felt this confident with a woman before. He had had relationships in the past but they always fizzled out after a few months and never went the way he thought they would from the get go. This was different. She was different.

"Am I gonna need a life jacket then or are you gonna rescue me?" She giggled again as she dialled a number into her mobile phone.

"I don't swim too well myself."

Tom sat in silence, grinning like a Cheshire cat as he watched David fail at even the most basic of flirting.

The taxi arrived just a few minutes later and David walked Molly down to the front door. He wanted to spend as much time in her presence as he could.

"I'll call you when I finish work and let you know what time I'll be picking you up at. It should be in the morning sometime." She said. Her voice was an octave lower and a little more serious than it had been upstairs.

"Yeah, that's fine. I can't wait." His voice trembled with anticipation. He was not sure whether he should hug her or kiss her as she left. He wanted to do both. It had been a while since he had been in this position. He could feel the closeness deep inside. The hairs on the back of his neck stood on end. Her huge eyes seemed to get even deeper. She held his gaze in a silent eternity until the taxi tooted the horn.

Molly turned her head toward the impatient driver for just a second and then back to David. She smiled a reluctant smile and then stepped toward him. She placed her lips against his, softly at first but then she eased off her pressure as if to pause and then kissed him more firmly, opening her mouth just enough for her to taste his lips. Without another word, she released herself from him, stepped away, smiled a coy smile and then skipped down the steps to the taxi.

David just watched her go. He felt a pang of disappointment as she climbed into the back of the taxi and waved, but at the same time he felt that fresh elation that a loving sensation brings. If he weighed it up too much his brain may have exploded, so he took the positive feeling back up to the flat with him and left any sadness at the door.

As he walked in to the room Tom gazed at him with that same wide Cheshire cat grin upon his face.

"Did you kiss her?"

"Er..Yeah!" David said trying to hide his smile.

"Good. I hope you have lots of babies and that they all look like her." Tom was genuinely happy for his friend but would never say that to his face because that would be too easy.

"Fuck off!" The words were said with a smile. The pair opened some more cans and chatted until sleep was the only option.

Chapter Thirty One

Phil Dobbs sat in his conservatory, a whiskey in one hand and a cigarette in the other. The air around him was filled with the smoke of a dozen cigarettes that he had chain smoked since arriving back home. His foot tapped in nervous anticipation of what may come his way.

In the car on the way back from the wake, he had received a text. The number had been withheld but who it came from was not as important as the message at this time. The message simply stated, "THEY ARE CHASING THE SHOTGUN".

The instant he had seen the text, panic gripped him and he could think of little else. The story was that John Hill's flat had been broken into and several items had been stolen, one of them being an antique shotgun. The robbery had been reported to the Police but as usual there were no leads or evidence to go on, and the investigation was dropped. It was hardly the crime of the century as the total value of the goods came to no more than a few thousand pounds. At the time the Kinsellas had been pulled in for it as they had recently been sacked from Hill's company. Jimmy and Billy both pleaded ignorance to the crime and they were later released without charge due to a lack of evidence.

There was a good reason that there was no evidence. There was no evidence because there was no robbery. The whole thing had been staged by Hill and Dobbs one afternoon. The flat had been empty at the time as Rachel had been working in the site office that morning, and Hill could not leave the site as there were deliveries to attend to. But Dobbs was able to be sent on errands for the whole day, running from the site to the builder's merchants but also to a lock-up at one of the nearby storage facilities.

The plan was that Dobbs would drop into the flat, stage a break in, make a mess of the place and hide the required items at the lock-up. The items were a laptop and the shotgun. If whoever was chasing the shotgun figured out that the robbery was staged then they could easily work out who had staged it.

Dobbs did not believe that his boss and long-time friend had been careless enough to fall from a building when there was no one else about and it would seem he was right, more or less. Now with the bizarre circumstances that surrounded Bailey's death, it looked like somebody was either trying to eliminate the old firm or keep something from being discovered.

Phil Dobbs may have been an integral part of the sub-organisation but he was not privy to the same information that the likes of Hill and Bailey would have been. He did what he was asked when he was asked and never pried into the reasons why. He believed that not knowing the details kept him safer than most. He could always plead ignorance to a third party or the police, but it would seem that a third party was involved, and ignorance may just get him killed.

Normally, the first person Dobbs would turn to was John Hill but with that no longer possible he was running on his own initiative.

First, he would need to get rid of the shotgun and the laptop, as that is what he thought would be the best thing to do. Hill had given Dobbs addresses to send the items too if something should happen to him but Dobbs was in no rush to move anything until he had received that text.

But now, time was of the essence.

Chapter Thirty Two

After several cans of beer and two action movies it was time for bed. Tom had rolled into bed and fallen asleep fully clothed on top of the covers and would remain that way until the morning.

David on the other hand, went to his room and stripped down to his boxer shorts. He lay under the covers with his hands tucked behind his head as he gazed at the ceiling with only thoughts of Molly drifting through his mind.

He thought of her large blue eyes, perfect white smile and the giggle in her voice when she seemed happy in his company. If he could picture a beautiful elven woman from a movie, then she was it with pixie like bobbed blonde hair and a flawless pale complexion.

There was a sense of joy in his heart that maybe he had found someone that might change his life. He did not want to dream the impossible dream just yet. The next few days would be crucial but David was looking forward to spending time with Molly.

Even with the sense of loss for his father, the overwhelming contentment he felt from spending time with her had somehow contained his grief. He had barely thought about the real reason he was in Bristol; supporting Rachel and attending a funeral. The distraction of Molly had pushed all his sadness to one side. There was no feeling that his father had died, but that a man that he had met a few years ago and was trying to build a close relationship with was now gone for good. He had managed nearly forty years without his father and although he had enjoyed the attachment that was starting to build, the last few years would never erase the abandonment that had shaped his life.

David settled back into the bed and felt the comforting veil of sleep descending on him. He prayed for nice dreams only as he pictured those eyes and that smile for one last time until his eyes slowly closed and sleep had him firmly within its grasp...

The sun shone brightly, almost blinding him in the warm summer glow it created. The Marina seemed somehow different, bigger and further reaching than he remembered but that was alright because the scene was amazing. The paths were wider and railings bigger, almost exaggerated. There was a hand tightly squeezing his as he walked along the bustling promenade of the town he called home, for he was no longer in Bristol. To his right was Molly; gone was the black suit that she had been wearing at the funeral. Now she was dressed in a short, flowing summer dress, her slightly tanned slim legs on show as she padded along in delicate fabric ballerinas.

There was the feeling of euphoria that only dreams have. Everyone that they met was either a good friend of David's or someone at the funeral. Everyone was smiling and dressed as brightly as the sun that shone in the brilliant blue, cloudless sky; its warmth filtering into every pore and every cell of his body.

As they continued to walk, the path seemed so much longer than it was in reality but then that is how dreams distort the fabric of reality and create an alternate universe for the dreamer to inhabit.

They stopped and turned to face each other. Her eyes were like sky, unnaturally blue and that smile had a heat all its own, warming his heart and the welling sense of solace that was now ever present.

As David looked in the direction they had come from, all the people they had passed had now disappeared. They were alone and the sun had quickly started to set, descending at an unnatural speed toward the horizon.

As he gazed at Molly, her face seemed so close that he could feel her breath on his cheek. She leaned further toward him and tilted her head to kiss him. He responded and wrapped his arms around her, enveloping her small frame.

Although they had only kissed for what felt like a minute, the sun was now gone. All the heat that had surrounded them had vanished. The sky grew dimmer, from a bright orange to deep purple and the air became still and cold. This did not stop Molly from kissing him. Their embrace increased in intensity. The passion flowed and their hands darted over each other's bodies. Within, David could feel his excitement grow and he knew regardless, whether this was a dream or reality, where this would lead. Even though they were outside, in public, the couple touched and explored the other.

Molly broke away and stopped kissing him. She pulled open his shirt and kissed down the front of his chest. He leaned back on to the nearby railings as she dropped to her knees in front of him. Swiftly, she undid his jeans and pulled them down. David threw his head back in ecstasy as she bore down on his engorged penis with her hot willing mouth. The sensation felt incredible but somewhere in his subconscious, it felt wrong. As his excitement increased, the cold air became freezing and uncomfortable on his skin. The only warmth was from Molly perched between his legs pleasuring him but now it seemed so wrong, what was happening to him....

His eyes flickered open in the darkness as he was ripped out of the dream. The coldness on his skin was the cold air as the duvet he had wrapped himself in was no longer on the bed at all. He looked down his body and could see a silhouetted figure lying between his legs, plunging their head deeply on to his erect member. He reached down to see if it was Molly as the dream had been but the bobbing head picked up the light from the room opposite through the open door. The hair was a deep shade of red. The figure lifted its head and tried to sit astride David's naked body, aiming to impale themselves on his penis.

"RACHEL?" The name was hushed but said with urgency.

"It's ok David, let it happen." Rachel's voice, still slightly slurred, answered him.

"NO! What are you doing?" He tried to buck her off.

"What we both want. I can see you want this too." She managed to raise herself once more and this time successfully mount David's prone body, his excited penis penetrated her fully.

"NO! NO! NO!" He reached out to lift her off but she forced him back, trying to grind her hips into him. He could still smell wine on her breath.

"Come on, fuck me!" She said in a low tone as she leaned ever closer to him to try and kiss his lips.

David managed to get his hands underneath her thighs and lifted her sideways as he spun away from under her. She fell onto the bed as David scrambled to his feet and reached for some clothes. In the dim light he could see his jeans. Swiftly he pulled them on.

"What do you think you are doing?" he asked.

"What I thought you wanted. What I need right now. I want you." She said on the brink of tears.

He looked down upon the beautiful mess that was Rachel. Her short hair kinked where she had slept on it and her makeup smudged around her eyes.

"It's not what I want. It's not what you should be doing either." He controlled his voice even though he was raging inside. "My father has been buried a matter of hours and you think this is ok?"

Rachel said nothing. She merely got off the bed and walked out of the room naked. Her face had a look of embarrassment but not of shame. It seemed clear that she was happy enough to force herself upon her dead partner's son but not deal with the rejection that inevitably followed. The door to the room opposite shut firmly behind her as she took refuge in the bedroom that she had shared until a week ago.

David closed his door and placed the one chair he had under the handle. There was no lock on the door and he did not trust her not to come in again. He stepped out of his jeans and put on a pair of shorts that he had packed with a drawstring and tied it tight, maybe it would offer him some protection if she anything again. Although, he doubted she would be able to look him in the eye again.

A glance at his phone told him it was nearly 3.30am. He dropped onto the bed and pulled the duvet from the floor. Sleep would take him once more but not for some time, as his brain tried to compute what had just happened. Once asleep, his dreams were no longer filled with images of Molly.

Chapter Thirty Three

It was still dark when Phil Dobbs left the house but as he approached the lock-up compound the black sky had turned into a deep blue-grey colour. The shape of the sun could just be seen through the thick blanket of cloud, yet it added very little light to the dawn.

He parked the car as close to main gates as possible. Paranoia gripped him to the point that he was almost too scared to set foot outside of his car. He reasoned with himself that the sooner he got out the sooner he would be finished and could get as far away as possible.

As he opened the door he heard a sound from the lane just over his shoulder. A drinks can fell or was kicked somewhere behind him. He pulled the door closed and stared wide eyed into the blackness. A moment later an urban fox scampered out onto the road from the lane. He paused for a minute longer, until the fox had disappeared and then quickly jumped from the car.

Either through haste or nervousness, the keys would not go into the large padlock that hung on the main gate. After what felt like an eternity, the key slipped in and the gates were open. Dobbs climbed back into the car and drove to the lock up.

A quick pan around with a torch told him the coast was clear or at least looked clear, so he took his chance and again jumped out of the car. He had parked so close that he accidentally swung the car door into the shutter. The dull sound echoed into the dim morning air. He cursed himself and looked around for any signs of life. There were none.

The shutter opened quicker than the front gate thankfully. He cast the torch light into the dim container and over the various pieces of small plant equipment. Behind boxes of tools and fixing kit was a cement mixer, half covered by a tarp. Hill had used it for some of the smaller jobs they were employed to do but now it had a different purpose.

Dobbs pulled back the tarp and reached in. He pulled out a laptop bag and then a rucksack. The bag contained the previously stolen laptop. The rucksack had the contingency plan; some cash and fake documentation, which included loaded credit cards under a false name, passports and a driver's licences.

He limped over to the car and dropped both items into the foot well of the passenger's seat. Once back inside the lock-up, he closed the shutter. Above his head in the rafters of the small concrete and wooden building was a gun box. A long wooden box with a handle on one side was within easy reach. Inside was John Hill's prized shotgun. The significance of which, Dobbs did not know but what he did know was that people were dying for it.

With the item firmly in hand, he lifted the shutter door. As the well-oiled, clanking metal rolled back above his head, the dawn was revealed in all its glory. The sun had finally broken through the morning cloud, glowing deep orange just above the horizon of the sleeping city. The black ominous shapes of the city centre buildings made the day feel all the more oppressive and spurred him to get the hell out of there. He also hoped Lorna was packing like he had asked her to. It was time for them to get away for a while. Although, for how long and to where was unknown.

Chapter Thirty Four

The dawn brought in its own brand of awkwardness. As soon as David was awake, he packed and dressed. He did not take a shower or look for Rachel. He grabbed his bag and went downstairs to kick Tom out of bed.

He entered the spare room as loudly as possible and pulled open the curtains after dumping his bag onto the bed.

"Wake up lazy bones." David said.

There was no response.

"Come on, it's raining women and fifty pound notes outside. Get up!"

Again no response.

David paused and looked at the lifeless heap under the duvet. There was no movement at all. Not even the rise and fall of a sleeping body breathing stirred beneath the tumble of bedding.

"Tom?" David's voice was quieter with concern and confusion.

Slowly he reached out and took his bag off the bed. Gripping the duvet, he gently pulled it toward him.

Still no movement.

His heart sank for a moment. Was something else going to happen? Again, he pulled the duvet toward him. He started to feel a pang of anxiety build up from his stomach. He felt a little sick and started to sweat. What was going on here?

With a quick swift pull, David whipped the duvet off the bed to reveal four pillows neatly arranged.

"MORNING!!!" Tom leapt out of the wardrobe, fully dressed. He then pushed David onto the bed and hit him with a pillow, repeatedly.

"YOU FUCKER!!" David shouted, angry but also relieved.

"Calm down Cochise, just a little early morning fun." Tom hit him with the pillow again.

"You're such a bastard!" David could not stay angry at his friend for too long regardless of the situation and started to laugh at him, also picking up a pillow and hitting him back.

"I'm your bastard brethren." Tom laughed back whilst being out of breath from the frenzied pillow attack.

"Yeah, yeah. Are you ready to go?" David was eager to get out of the house and escape the incident from the early hours of that morning.

"Almost, aren't we having breakfast here?"

"No. Change of plan; let's go to the café downtown. Rachel's out of it and I don't want to disturb her. I'll give a Molly a bell to tell her where to meet us." David was in a hurry.

"Rachel ain't out of it, she's in the lounge. She's been awake for hours."

David's heart sank again, this time for a very real reason. He did not want to come face to face with her again but there was no escaping it now.

"Are you packed?" David asked.

"Yeah, yeah,"

"Say goodbye to her and then take the bags to the car. I'll be there in a minute." David thrust his bag into his friend's arms and pushed him through the door.

David stood for a minute and listened until he heard Tom descending the stairs down to street level. Once he heard the front door open and close, he walked slowly into the lounge. Rachel was sat on the sofa dressed in just a dressing gown and looking out of the window. A mug of coffee sat steaming away. A lit cigarette burning slowly in the ashtray, it was the first time he had seen Rachel smoke.

"We're off now." He piped up to get her attention.

She merely turned her head and smiled a disappointed smile. There was a long, uncomfortable pause. David smiled a fake smile and turned to go.

"Wait!" Rachel said.

He stopped and turned back but stood by the door.

"I've got something for you." She stood up and her dressing gown fell open revealing her naked breasts, a toned stomach with a belly button ring and thin lacey panties that covered very little. She walked across to the cabinet and pulled out a small photo album, then walked over to David. She did nothing to cover her modesty.

"What is it?" He asked, averting his eyes from the body before him that a few hours ago pressed against him.

"Just some photos, mostly of just you and Jay, he wanted you to have them." She handed him the album.

"Thank you, genuinely." He said. It was the most sincere thing he had ever said to her.

"I think he knew something was going to happen. He gave me that after your last visit and told me to give it to you." She looked directly at him but could not hold his gaze.

Flicking open to the inside cover, he looked down at the first picture of he and his father together. It was a baby picture that David had never seen before. His father must have only been seventeen in the photo, skinny and fresh faced. He turned over the next page to a photo of their first meeting as adults about two years ago, Rachel had taken the picture.

"Thank you again," He said to her with a genuine smile on his face this time, "This means a lot."

"Your Dad said you should look beyond the photos and see your future."

David looked at her strangely, that was a weird thing to say he thought. He smiled at her and turned to leave.

"You can still come and visit, if you want." The words were said with some expectation.

"Take care Rachel, I'm sorry for your loss." Then he left. He did not know whether he would ever see her again but deep down he prayed he would not.

Chapter Thirty Five

Jimmy banged his large tanned fist on the door. It was early but he did not care. He wanted to know what the hell was going on before he ended up with a bullet in him or worse. He thought of leaving Billy in the van just in case. Although, just in case of what? If something happened in the house, Billy would still try to rescue his brother and then probably meet the same fate.

As a rule Jimmy always wanted Billy to be as far away from trouble as possible unless there was a requirement for violence, then he was the only person Jimmy trusted to watch his back.

The door opened and he was greeted by Ducty dressed in a tracksuit and a baseball hat. It was as if Ducty geared his clothing choice to look like a stereotypical small time drug dealer.

"What do you want, Jimmy?" There was no good morning just a question.

"I wanna talk about all this shit that's happening." Jimmy uttered in neutral tones.

"You'd better come in." Ducty stood back from the door to let Jimmy through. He glanced toward the van parked in the street to see Billy stepping out from the passenger seat. Ducty caught his eye and shook his head, to show he was not welcome then shut the door, not waiting to see if the other brother would do as he was told and stay in the van.

"What the fuck is going on?" the neutral tones had now left Jimmy's voice.

"I told you already. There is a professional at work on the patch and he's going through the old firm. You need to keep your ear to the ground and eyes open. Speak to those who may know something and do what you can to keep yourself alive." Ducty spoke in a calm voice. He was not the typical local criminal. He was articulate and intelligent. Ducty never used violence or threatened violence to get what he needed to get done. To many, his level of calmness was frightening enough, almost psychopathic.

"Yeah, but you must know fuckin…." Jimmy's voice was raised.

"SHUT YOUR MOUTH! Keep it together and do your own digging. Do not think you can come here and expect me to hand you all the answers because that is not going to happen." It was the first time that Jimmy had seen a break in the ever calm persona of Ducty. "You go ask the questions about who and why on your own time. Do not come here and start to waste mine."

Jimmy measured his next question before he asked it. He knew that on the surface Ducty looked like a small timer but was far more connected than he let on. If you told Ducty a secret, it stayed a secret. Jimmy had once before raised his voice to Ducty and when he raised his voice to most people they sat up and took notice with an undertone of fear but not

Ducty, he merely listened intently and then gave his opinion on that occasion.

"Do ya know about the shotgun?" Jimmy said in a far more controlled manner.

"I know that it's the reason for the chaos. Do you know where it is?" Ducty's voice had returned to an average volume.

"I thought it had been stolen."

"It has not been stolen. That much I do know. But I think Jay staged the robbery for everyone to think he didn't have it anymore." Ducty's logic was sound.

"But why? What's the point? I didn't think it was worth much. Duncs said…" Jimmy was interrupted again.

"Duncan played you. Did he not tell you to try and find the shotgun?"

"Yeah, but as a favour to Jay." Jimmy looked confused.

"Do you really think Duncan would be doing favours for Jay? The last favour Jay did was taking you and that fucking retard of a brother of yours on, and then you rob the place and get sacked."

There was a vicious pause before the reply. Jimmy hated it when people insulted Billy. Yes, he was slow but not retarded. Jimmy often defended his younger sibling in this kind of situation but this time. Ducty was right, Billy had got them sacked for not doing as he was told.

"Don't call my broth..."

"Or what, Jimmy? Are you going to kick my head in? If you and that sack of shit sat outside used your fucking heads instead of your fists once in a while then maybe you wouldn't be in a pile of shit all the time." The words were meant to sting as they were said, provoking Jimmy into action.

"YOU CUNT!!!" Jimmy reached out and gripped Ducty by the throat, pinning him against the wall but instead of the panic that others displayed when attacked by the bigger and more viscous Kinsella brother, Ducty just took the move and then reached his arms out to match Jimmy's stance and pushed him back. Although Ducty was the smaller man, he was also younger and more agile. Jimmy had never placed his hands on the drug dealer before so he had never felt how wiry and strong he was. Jimmy tried to punch his opponent in the face but was blocked by the younger man's taught arms. Ducty released the grip of his right hand and jabbed the burly scrapper in the throat. Jimmy let go and his hands were instinctively raised to his own neck, the blow stunning him briefly. By the time he regained his composure to counter the attack he had already lost. Ducty stood pointing an automatic pistol at his chest.

"Now calm the fuck down." The placid voice had returned to the drug dealer.

"Are you gonna fucking shoot me?" There were no nerves in the question only defiance.

"Don't be stupid, but the way you are going somebody else will. If you want to buy yourself out of the hole you are digging for yourself you need to get that shotgun. You've been played by Duncan. It got him killed and it's going to get you killed unless you get to that gun."

Some of the pennies had started to finally drop for the elder Kinsella brother. Duncan had told Jimmy about the missing shotgun and said that it was valuable but Jimmy had naturally thought in terms of money. Clearly there was another agenda. The brothers had been employed to work on the construction site by John Hill at the request of Bailey. Hill and Bailey's relationship had gone back a lot of years, that was no secret but when the Kinsellas had entered the picture twenty plus years ago Bailey was near the top of the pile within the criminal classes and Hill worked for him. After a decade or so, Bailey had lost his importance. Some say it had to do with the introduction of the Kinsellas as hired muscle. Both were loose cannons but Bailey thought it was better to have them on side rather than an obstacle to negotiate in the future. Duncan Bailey was not ruthless, he was a shrewd operator but taking on the brothers may have been the reason for his tumble from the top of the pile.

John Hill on the other hand was a hardworking man regardless of the activity. Legitimate or illegal, Hill always gave his best and that carried more favour with the powers that be. The criminal underworld was akin to a tree; deep seated roots at its foundation but only as strong as its many branches. As the years had passed Bailey's branch had become a fragile twig bending with the slightest breeze, but Hill had kept his nose clean and become part of the powerful trunk that held the whole organisation together, feeding its many limbs.

Unlike Bailey, Hill was a good man at heart and he had just fallen into his position within the organisation. He knew that once he was in, it was difficult to leave but Hill figured that keeping his head down and his mouth shut would prove to be fruitful in the long run; he was not wrong.

Whatever their places on the pecking order, both the men were now dead and the reason was still unknown. There were plenty of questions that needed asking and there were not too many people close to either man to ask. If Bailey knew anything, Jimmy thought that he would have been informed but now the doubts were creeping in.

"Who should I ask?" Jimmy said. His eyes flitting between the handgun and Ducty's face, trying to read what would happen next.

"Use your head, Jimmy." Ducty was cool and seemed quite relaxed with the firearm in his hand.

"Rachel?" It was who he thought of first.

"I said use your head not your dick." Ducty rolled his eyes.

"Dobbs?"

"See, there is something in that dense skull of yours." A smug smile widened across the drug dealer's face. "I suggest you start there. And Jimmy, Keep it off the streets, OK!"

It was some friendly advice from someone who was not exactly a friend; an associate maybe but not a friend.

As Jimmy turned to leave with his tail tucked firmly between his legs, he decided he would ask the question that was now nagging at him, instead of letting it fester away and grow into something else.

"When did you grow such big balls?"

"I've always had big balls Jimmy. You just thought I worked for you and Duncs but I'm employed by many people." The handgun was still firmly pointing forward.

"I had you down as small time." It was a cheap shot but Jimmy took it.

"If I look small time, it's because I want to look small time. You think about all shit that gone down this week, then small time is going to get overlooked and that's probably why you haven't taken a bullet yet." Again the words stung Jimmy.

"You got any gear on you now?"

"I don't think a tenners worth of weed is going to help you find the shooter, is it?" Ducty said sarcastically.

"It's for Billy." Jimmy lied.

Ducty reached into his jacket pocket with his left hand not to lower the handgun and threw it at Jimmy.

"Whatever it takes to stop him licking the windows eh?" Ducty smiled through the insult. "That's on the house by the way."

Jimmy just sneered back and opened the door to leave but turned back one last time.

"Are we ever gonna do business again?"

"If you find that shotgun you won't need to scrape up your milk money to buy gear from me."

"Is it that valuable?" Jimmy asked.

"It's valuable to the right people."

"Why aren't you interested in it?"

Ducty paused before he answered. He did not know the true value of the shotgun but it was not the monetary value that was of interest. The true value was what it contained and Ducty did not know what that was.

"Let's put it this way, all the minor deals I did with you and Duncs put diesel in my Audi and food on my table. But the people who employed Jay are the ones looking for it and my deals with them bought my Audi and the house that my table stands in. You never bite the hand that feeds you Jimmy. Jay Hill did, look what happened." Ducty had clearly had enough of Jimmy Kinsella and ushered him out without another word.

Jimmy lit up a cigarette as he walked back to the van. If he was to crawl his way out of the gutter and from under the shadow of his former mentor, then he would have to get his hands on the weapon. He was known for how ruthless he could be but now everything would have to go to the next level. This was Jimmy's time to shine.

Chapter Thirty Six

David watched as Tom put the last forkful of food into his mouth and pushed the empty, grease covered plate, across the table.

"Do you worry about your heart?" David asked.

"No more than you worry about your dress sense." Tom winked as he chewed the last morsels of his Olympic breakfast.

"What's wrong with my clothes now?" David's voice went up an octave as he replied to the jibe.

"Well I know you were born in the seventies but I didn't think your wardrobe was." Tom took a big swig of tea to clean his palate for the next insult.

David looked down at the surfer style t-shirt he wore that had been deliberately aged to give that worn-in look.

"I only bought this last week!"

"Yeah, but from which charity shop?" Tom fired back.

"Does it matter?" David said resigning to the fact that he could not win against the razor sharp sarcasm of his best friend.

"It does if you're trying to impress that girl whilst not making it obvious that you are quite a bit older than her."

Tom winked again and then glanced over his friend's shoulder, "And here she is."

David craned his neck to see Molly crossing the road. She simply wore a loose fitting purple vest top, jeans and a pair of canvas shoes. It mattered not what she wore, David was captivated. He had been struggling to remember what she looked like just moments ago. One of those rare things that when you try to see the image of someone's face with your mind and the part of your brain that should easily recall such memory engrams decides that those files are now off limits. He was secretly pleased that she was as beautiful as he had thought; brain functioning normally or not.

"Don't blow in your pants now, old man." Tom said as he raised the large white mug to his lips to drain the last of his tea.

"You're such a dickhead." David countered.

"I'm your dickhead, brethren."

David did not reply. He merely turned to watch Molly walk gracefully across the café. It was like they were part of a story telling music video and Molly was the muse. David's malfunctioning brain almost put music to her moves.

"Morning boys," she said with confidence. She dropped into the empty seat next to David and looked at his empty plate. "Are you good to go David?"

"Did you want a tea or a coffee before we set off?" He asked out of courtesy.

"I'm good thanks. I popped in with the olds before I came here so they won't miss me too much." A brief glimpse of bemusement flashed across her face and then it was gone. "But I don't think they'll miss me too much. They were packing too."

"They must need a holiday." Tom piped up.

"If you say so," She said dismissively, "Shall we go? I'm eager to see all these beaches you told me about."

"Let's go then." David said, unable to contain the smile on his face as his friend was blanked by the pretty girl in favour of him.

They stood in unison and left the café together. After a few bits of chit chat on the pavement and a promise to meet up for a drink that night, they went their separate ways. Tom to his car and David followed Molly to hers. All three were oblivious to the fact that they were being watched.

As the door of the café closed behind the group, the man looked up from his newspaper. Luckily he had been unobserved but that's how it was supposed to be. Jones had dressed in work clothes; Steel toe capped boots, ripped jeans and a paint speckled hoodie. His face was covered by the paper he read and the baseball cap that was pulled down to the level of his eyes.

He watched them talk just outside and wished he could hear their plans but for now they were not his concern as his phone started to vibrate in his pocket. He retrieved the phone and looked at the display. The number was withheld.

"Yes." Jones answered the phone.

"If I told you to follow the brothers would you know what I meant?" The same accent free, emotionless voice that always delivered the jobs echoed at the other end of the line.

"I would." Some late night research had revealing Jimmy K on Flynn's phone as Jimmy Kinsella, a name he already knew. The Kinsellas has never been subtle. Even if others did not know them personally, the Kinsellas were infamous.

"Then you have the next part of the job. Learn what you can and dispose of what you have to. Understood?"

"Understood." The line went dead.

Regardless of what he found out, Jones knew he was tying off all the loose ends. He knew the drill all too well. But he would take a detour first.

Chapter Thirty Seven

The hot liquid powered over her body. There was only so much soap and water could do. Some things can never be washed off. Dirt and grime take little effort, just fresh water and pressure, then everything is clean again. Shame can never be washed off. Not even after a thousand showers, there are some stains that will never be erased. To everyone else there is nothing there but Rachel always knew where the secret blemishes were; imperfections of a flawed past.

The shower felt good but there was a fresh indignity to add to all the others she had tried so many years to cover up. Attempting to sleep with David was yet another mistake she would regret to her dying day. All she needed was to feel wanted again. John Hill had wanted her, so had Bailey. Both were dead.

She had been scraping a living as a stripper and pole dancer when Hill walked into her life. He had been drinking but was not drunk. She on the other hand, had downed half a bottle of vodka over the course of that evening. It had affected her more than normal as she was not able to buy food that day after using the last of her money on the alcohol and two packs of cigarettes which she would chain smoke over a few hours. Her entire life consisted of either earning money to buy vices, or earning money to buy herself out of trouble.

Hill could see she was vulnerable and made his move, not because she was easy but because it was the right thing to do, he got her out of a tight spot. After a brief courtship, Hill invited her to live with him in his flat. She had gladly accepted his offer and even stopped dancing when he asked. He became her benefactor, lover and friend; none of which she had ever had before.

Rachel never talked about her past to him. She never talked about the dancing and some of the 'extras' she had to do. Never did she talk about other ways she used to make money either. Although she had never stooped low enough to walk the streets, she did the occasional stag party strip-o-gram, and again there might be extras offered. She never talked about the parties with the few casual friends she did have. Nor would she talk about the extra hundred quid she made from the queue that formed after she agreed to perform oral sex on the groom and the best man when the party got out of hand. But her logic was to agree to something she would do willingly, instead of having something forced upon her.

Jimmy Kinsella tried to force himself upon her on more than one occasion. The first time, the strip club bouncer had to step in which turned into a fist fight between the two men and Rachel had managed to slip away. The second time, a few weeks later, when John Hill was her knight in shining armour and that was catalyst for their relationship.

Jimmy had cornered Rachel in a dark corridor near to the fire exit where she would often escape to smoke a cigarette between dances. He grabbed her by the arm and dragged her into the alley at the back of the club. She had never felt so alone or scared in her life before. His whiskey breath filled her senses and his rough hands pawed at her flesh. No matter how she tried to get around him he kept pulling her back and forcing her up against the wall of that cold, damp, dark alley. The icy brickwork burned against her near naked flesh and the heat of Kinsella's probing hands did nothing to warm her. She could scream but nobody would hear her over the booming music and the communal areas of the club were on the other side of the dance floor. The only people to come out here were those trying to be alone or those up to no good; they were there for both, she the former, and he the latter.

Rachel almost resigned herself to the impending assault until she heard a voice from the doorway.

"Jimmy! Leave the lady alone." It was John Hill.

Jimmy stopped what he was doing and turned to see who was interrupting his fun.

"FUCK OFF JAY!" Jimmy raged; his fists clenched ready to be used if needed.

"I can't do that Jimmy. It wouldn't be right." Hill was calm and unfazed by the angry man.

Rachel seized her opportunity and ran past Jimmy and back into the club but instead of running to the bouncers as she usually would, she stood next to her saviour.

"You stay out of my shit in future." Jimmy spat the words directly into Hill's face, then barged passed him to return to the club.

"Gladly Jimmy, gladly," Hill placed a protective arm around Rachel as they both watched the furious brother storm off. From that moment on, Rachel was never far from John Hill's side.

They had many happy years together and a few not so happy ones. Her old habits often came back to haunt her. She would, on occasion, cheat on Hill. Sometimes with a random bloke she met at the pub or, as the case had been a few times, with Duncan Bailey. It hurt him, but Hill forgave her more than once. She counted herself lucky.

Her actions had created so much heartache but she tried her best to change. The happiest she had ever seen her partner was once he had found his son. David had made Hill's life complete and changed the man for the better. But his untimely death had spoiled what should have been a perfect year for them as a family, small and unusual as they were, but a family all the same.

Rachel felt it was almost instinctive to try and couple with David, after all he was the younger version of the man who had taken care of her for so many years but she was wrong and her decision had burned her good. David had turned tail and ran from her. Rachel was alone and she had never felt as vulnerable as she did right then.

She switched off the shower and stepped out to dry herself. The waves of isolation and sorrow came and went like the rising tide, each one bringing more grief until she was almost out of her depth. Dropping to her knees with nothing but the towel around her she sobbed her heart out. As each tear fell, the tide of sorrow eased. Eventually she was all cried out and able to drag herself from the bathroom floor.

With panties and a dressing gown on, she descended to the floor below and put on the kettle. One day at a time she told herself, as she pulled a mug from the kitchen cupboard. She reached for the coffee jar but did not manage to remove the lid as she was interrupted by the front door buzzer.

"Hello?" She spoke into the intercom confused at who would be calling so early.

"Hi. I'm an old friend of Jay's. I've come to pay my respects." The male voice said.

"The funeral was yesterday."

"Yeah, I know. I'm sorry I missed it. I have flowers." There was an insistence in the voice.

"What's your name?" Rachel asked.

"Jones. Robbie Jones, I'm sure Jay must have mentioned me before."

Rachel thought for a moment and then buzzed him up. 'How bad could it be?' she thought to herself. How bad indeed?

Chapter Thirty Eight

After the morning traffic congested escape from the heart of the city, the couple started to relax into the journey. With two and something hours of open road to cover, they settled into the small talk and the 'getting to know each other' conversation. David could not believe how comfortable he felt in Molly's company. Twenty-Four hours ago they were strangers but now the words flowed between them like old friends.

"I've met you before." Molly said.

"Really, when?" David's brain went into search mode, trying to think why he could not remember such a meeting.

"A few months back. You came to stay with Jay and Rachel and you guys were in the Indian." She paused to see if the penny would drop.

"Ah, I remember now. You came over and said 'Hi'. You were with another pretty girl with red hair." He smiled and laughed with a realisation that their connection, no matter how brief, went back further than yesterday morning.

"My older sister, she lives in Australia. She's a model. She was back for a few weeks."

"Oh wow! That's great." He literally had nothing to say.

"It's ok. Most people get missed when they meet Sinead. She's beautiful." She giggled that sweet child-like giggle at his obvious embarrassment.

"She is but those looks run in the family for sure." David internally praised his own recovery.

"Why thank you kind sir." She replied.

"That's cool, you dad is a good looking man," He said it with his tongue firmly in his cheek.

"You're such a douche." She smiled as she said it. Molly seemed comfortable that kind of banter with the male of the species. The connection between them was instant she could feel it and she knew David could as well. Lucky in love was something Molly had never experienced. Yes, she was beautiful and yes, she was charming but it had only attracted men that either wanted her as a trophy or wanted to control her. After being cheated on by one and beaten by another, she had decided to give men a wide berth for a while.

Her last boyfriend, Joe, was a typical player; good looking, charming and fit but he loved women as much as he loved himself. He could have been a character written in to a soap opera or a bad sit-com he was that much of a stereotype. Molly had been able to predict his lies and knew from his behaviour that she was not his prime concern anymore. So she ended the relationship thinking it was what he wanted. They had not been seeing each other for very long, just a few months, so Molly thought it would be an easy break up with very little drama, maybe some disappointment but perhaps a relief for them both. That was not the case at all.

When she broached the subject of them going their separate ways but remaining friends the reaction she got was completely unpredicted. Joe accused her of seeing someone else and that was the reason for her decision to break it off. Molly was completely sideswiped by this response.

She tried to explain that there was nobody else, and that her intention was to end their relationship while there was no bitterness or resentment between them. Joe's mood took a turn for the worse. He became aggressive.

Molly was not used to that from any boyfriend she had had previously. Her next mistake was to get up to leave the flat. He gripped her arm hard and pulled back toward him, then pushed her back down onto the sofa. Stunned and frightened, Molly felt trapped without many options to escape. She pleaded with him just to let her go and not to harm her, but the now very vulnerable Molly redirected Joe's demeanour from aggressive to nasty. He thrived on Molly's apparent helplessness and fear.

As tears ran down her cheeks, Joe started to shout inches from her face. Telling her that she would never find better than him, how inadequate she had been as a girlfriend and how she had been cheated on and dumped so many times before because she was useless. None of this was true; not in Molly's eyes. She pushed him away and tried to leave again. He slapped her, not once but twice across her face, the second strike catching her nose which started to bleed profusely.

The sight of an injured, distraught young woman did not deter Joe. He grew angrier at the blood that was dripping over his sofa and grabbed her by the hair, dragging the pitiful figure of Molly to the floor. As she lay broken and crying in a heap on the carpet, trying not to drip blood anywhere else, the short summer dress she had chosen to wear had ridden up exposing her thighs and the thin panties that she wore. Joe decided that he would teach her the ultimate lesson in thinking that she could possibly be the one to dump him and leapt onto her body.

Trying to keep her face down on the floor, he was no longer concerned about blood on the carpet, but struggled to pin her to the carpet while undoing his jeans.

Molly knew what was coming next and this was not going to happen while she could help it. She could feel her panties pulled to one side as her assailant tried to penetrate her. Somewhere inside her fragile body, Molly found the strength to raise her upper body from the floor, dislodging her attacker. Joe tried to regain his dominance by lifting himself further up her body. This brought his face into close proximity to the rear of Molly's skull. She thrust her head back and caught Joe perfectly on the bridge of the nose, breaking it instantly.

He fell back, writhing in agony, his own nose now pouring with blood. Molly got to her feet and pulled her clothes back into place. Instead of taking the opportunity to flee, she turned to look down at the pathetic display at her feet. Joe had tears streaming from his eyes mixing with the blood from his nose. His now flaccid penis hung from the zip of his jeans, exposed and vulnerable as Molly had been. In an act of empowerment she stamped her foot down hard between Joe's legs. He gave a high pitched whimper and curled into a ball. As she turned to go, Molly decided to leave her now ex-boyfriend with a parting thought to mull over as he tried to recover.

"Don't you ever come near me again! You know the kind of people my father deals with so if I so much as see you in the same street, then I will let him know what you tried to do here." Her words were spoken with venom but not screamed.

About a week later Joe was found beaten unconscious in a park in the Fishponds area of Bristol. He had missing teeth, a broken jaw, a fractured wrist and a ruptured testicle. He left the city once he had recovered.

Molly knew full well the kind of people that her father had dealings with, in work and out. She was wise to all the criminal activities that had occurred before she was born and everything that had happened more recently. Phil Dobbs never kept secrets from his family, regardless of the situation but he never told Molly he had sussed that Joe was the reason for the bruises on her face, he had taken the matter into his own hands and paid Pete Flynn a hundred quid to 'wound but not kill' Joe. When she heard about the beating she knew her father had instigated it but it was never spoken about.

She had decided that she would steer clear of men for a while. But that while turned into two years of the occasional date from which nothing came of. The 'Joe' incident seemed to get around and the eligible young men of the city did not wish the same treatment, so her single life was not entirely her own choice.

Meeting David was refreshing. He did not know all about the illicit goings on that surrounded his father or the building firm that he ran and owned. She hoped that he would not find out the darkest secrets, and that way the memories of his father, brief as they were, would be of a good man. Which if she was being completely honest, would be true.

John 'Jay' Hill was not a bad man and from what she had seen so far, his son was the same. Molly knew that the circumstances that brought them together had not been due to an industrial accident. She was smart enough to see beyond the façade of the events. This is why she had suggested going to stay with David. To get away from whatever or whoever had decided to devastate the business. Molly hoped that together they could escape whatever would happen next. The reality was there was no escape, only a delaying of the inevitable.

Chapter Thirty Nine

Jones casually walked out of the property just thirty minutes after he had walked in. He peeled off the latex gloves he had been wearing and tucked them into his jeans pocket. He faced little resistance from Rachel. She seemed resigned to her fate, almost welcomed it.

When he walked into the flat he was armed with nothing more than a bunch of flowers and his bare hands, which were dangerous enough. Rachel greeted and invited him in. She gave a nonchalant thank you for the flowers and took them from him.

"How do…sorry…how did you know Jay?" She asked putting the flowers into a vase, trying to look as if she had no time at all.

"He used to send some business my way." Jones said. He was not lying.

"You knew him well then?" Rachel asked while clipping the ends off the stems of the flowers, she was failing to give the impression that this was something she was well practiced at.

"Not really." He walked into the kitchen area uninvited.

"So why are you here?" She stopped what she was doing and began to grow uncomfortable.

"I need some information." He was now only a few feet from Rachel and there was nowhere she could go to except through him.

"I...I don't know anything." Her voice broke with the rapidly rising anxiety that was starting to overwhelm her.

"Of course you do. Where is the shotgun?" His voice was calm like he was asking for a cup of coffee from a burger van.

"That was stolen."

"We both know that's not the truth." Again calm.

"Will you please leave?" Rachel said in a futile show of strength to this stranger.

Jones casually took a steak knife from the knife block on the counter top and stood directly in front of the trembling Rachel.

"You are going to tell me what I want to know. I'm asking nicely but unless you start talking to me it will become unpleasant very quickly." His voice had stepped up to just above neutral which made the threat in his words seem so much more intimidating. If he was this calm while threatening someone, what would he be saying or doing if he was raging?

Rachel shook her head but no words formed on her lips. There was no protest from her. She was defeated.

"I will ask again. Where is the shotgun?" He voice was calm again.

"I-I..d-don't know." Rachel was pale and her trembling was almost uncontrollable.

"Who has it?"

"I..s-said I d-dont…" The words could not escape her mouth.

"BULLSHIT!!" He screamed into her face. Jones grabbed her by her short hair and forced her through the flat to the family bathroom. He lifted her in his powerful arms and dropped her into the bath. She started to gasp for breath as the horror of her situation escalated.

Jones dropped the plug into the hole and switched on both taps hot and cold taps. The bath filled rapidly. Rachel started to kick out in panic but Jones placed the blade under her chin. She froze.

"Tell me what I want to know and I promise I'll be out of here quickly." He was not calm any more but he did not shout at her again.

"I d-don't know where it is. B-but I d-do know who took it." She found the strength to speak.

"Now that wasn't so hard now was it?" His calm voice returned. He removed the blade from her throat and turned off the cold tap but left the hot tap running. "So who took it? You can tell me."

The warm water started to circulate around the bath tub and gave Rachel a modicum of comfort in her predicament.

"Phil Dobbs! Phil Dobbs took it." She spat the words out.

"Did he take anything else?" His voice had the patronising tone of a bad schoolteacher talking down to a frightened child.

"A laptop" That was all she knew so that was all she could say.

"Do you know what was on it?"

Rachel just shook her head, praying that there would be no more questions and this man would leave her alone.

"Are you lying to me?" He asked as he turned off the hot tap. The bath was now three quarters full of water. Rachel's skin looked red as if the temperature was too much for her, but she did not protest, she just laid semi naked in the bath and shook her head. Her sad looking blue eyes told a tale all their own. One of a damaged individual that had been rescued once before from the sharks of the criminal underworld only to be cast out into the big scary sea for one last time.

"Are you right handed?" Jones asked her in that patronising tone he had perfected for when speaking to terrified soul under his control.

Rachel looked confused but nodded her answer.

Jones lifted her left forearm out of the water and placed the steak knife against her wrist. She flinched put could not pull her arm from him.

"It's ok I'm not going to hurt you." He lied.

Jones drew the serrated edge of the blade across her skin, deep enough to break the surface and draw a little blood but no deeper. He started at the outside edge of her wrist again and dragged the metal teeth across her skin once more. Again and again, he slowly sliced into her flesh but each cut was no more than a scratch. Once there were a dozen or so thin red lines in her skin, Jones stopped.

"Did you know that when someone slashes their wrists, there are often hesitation marks and their wrists often look like this" Jones lifted Rachel's left forearm and showed her his work.

Her eyes just glazed with the fear of what was to follow.

"But that didn't hurt did it? No, of course not!" His voice was changing pitch as he seemed to breathe deeper, preparing himself for what he was about to do. "I said I wouldn't hurt you didn't I?"

Rachel nodded for the last time.

"Well, I lied!" Jones pinned her arm to side of the bath and then plunged the knife deep into the centre of her forearm, the blade penetrating neatly between the bones and piercing the other side. In a swift action he drew the knife down towards her hand, the blade skipped and bumped over the bones of her wrist as she screamed in shock. Jones pushed her wounded arm into the burning water and held her rigid body, the liquid quickly changed to a deep crimson. The heat made the blood flow so much quicker. In what seemed like only a few seconds, Rachel moved no more. She had quickly succumbed to the blood loss.

Jones held his position for a few moments and then relaxed his grip on the lifeless figure. A fingertip touch on the right side of Rachel's limp neck barely detected a pulse, death was a certainty. As a measure of routine, Jones checked the room and the rest of the flat for any trace of his presence. His technique had been perfected over years and again it was flawless.

He walked back into the bathroom and placed a finger on Rachel's neck once more. No pulse. Jones smiled to himself, not of joy but one of satisfaction of a job well done.

"Heartbroken girlfriend takes her own life after partner falls from building." He said out loud, "That's too long a headline." He continued his solo conversation as he left the flat but stopped as he walked into street. He just had to find Phil Dobbs and then the brothers but he had the feeling that if he found one he might find them all.

Chapter Forty

Phil and Lorna Dobbs packed as much as they could into one large suitcase and a couple of holdalls. They were not sure how long they would be gone for or whether they would ever come back. Dobbs had gotten rid of the items as instructed and now had to get rid of himself and his wife. Molly was already away and safe, for now. When the time was right, Phil would message his daughter and tell her the plan.

"The car is packed, can you be ready in five minutes." Dobbs shouted upstairs to his wife.

Lorna appeared at the top of the stairs in just her underwear and a dressing gown, no make-up and bed hair.

"I'll do my best, have we got every…." The sentence was interrupted by the crash of the front door flying open.

Billy Kinsella stood in the doorway, in his hands a police door opening battering ram. He dropped it onto the floor and made a grab for Dobbs. Billy was taller and stockier than the wiry Irish man.

"What the fuck do you want?" Dobbs said under protest.

"It's what you have." Jimmy's harsh voice roared in behind his brother as he entered the house. Jimmy glanced up the stairs to see the half-naked Lorna at the top of the stairs, "Morning Lorna, no need to get dressed on my account." And he launched himself up the stairs as she ran for the bedroom.

The internal door was no match for Jimmy, Lorna shut it and flicked the catch to lock it but the hinges ripped off at the door frame as Jimmy kicked it through. He grabbed her by her short hair and threw her on to the bed.

"Billy, bring Dobbs here." He shouted down to his brother without looking away from the prone figure on the bed. He eyed the woman. Only thin material covered her modesty.

The commotion of the struggle on the stairs echoed in the high ceiling hallway and only ceased when Dobbs was eventually dumped through the doorway. He lifted his eyes toward his wife, who was lying on the bed face up with Jimmy Kinsella's hand firmly pressed against her throat whilst he sat beside her.

"Don't you fucking touch her Jimmy!" Dobbs screamed at the man who pawed his wife.

"Or what? Or what, Dobbs? What are you going to do?" Jimmy's voice was too calm for comfort.

"What do you want?" Dobbs asked.

"Where is the stuff?" Billy piped up.

"Yeah Phil, where's the stuff?" Jimmy laughed at the stricken man while his hand now stroked Lorna's skin, his uninvited fingertips touching her face and neck.

"It's gone." Dobb's eyes darted between his wife and Jimmy, not knowing what the next move would be.

"Gone where?" Billy asked.

"Yeah Phil, gone where?" No laughter or eye contact from the man on the bed. Jimmy watched as his hands slowly moved over the lacy bra of the frightened woman. Her body flinched as he obviously touched her nipple through the thin material but she remained silent the whole time.

"I've sent it away." Dobb's swallowed hard, "But I can get it, just let her go. She knows nothing."

"I'm sure she knows lots of tricks and she's dressed right for her best ones I bet." Jimmy's voice was low with a hint of nervous anticipation as he traced his fingers along the length of Lorna's belly and stopped just at the edge of the fabric of her panties.

"Don't do this Jimmy, I beg you." Dobb's had tears in his eyes.

"Molly is more my type but she's not here is she." Jimmy looked pitifully at the pleading husband who looked physically smaller with each passing moment, his spirit diminishing with the nightmare caused by the evil of the brothers.

"Don't Jimmy, I can get the stuff."

"Where've you sent it?" Jimmy asked, more forcefully this time, his hands now stroking Lorna's legs.

"I sent it to Jay's son, couriered it this morning. Now let her go, please Jimmy." Dobbs drooled like a distressed child. He was not a hard man by any means in fact quite the opposite and he had been carried into the criminal world through association and not by desire. His loyalty to Hill had kept him from harm's way all these years but now there was nobody to watch over him. He reached into his pocket and retrieved the courier slip to prove that he spoke the truth and threw it toward Jimmy, feebly.

"This won't arrive til tomorrow," Jimmy said, staring at the documentation, "but it does have the address." Jimmy stood up, tucking the receipt into his back pocket and took his attention away from Lorna. He reached down lifting Dobbs from the floor by his collar, almost choking the man.

"You got what you want, now please leave her alone." Dobbs pleaded again, his sullen eyes glued to the floor, not wishing to anger Jimmy at all.

"Don't worry Phil, I'm not going to touch her." Jimmy said reaching into his pocket. He pushed the older man out through the broken door and lobbed a small box of condoms at Billy, "I'm not, but he will." casting a thumb toward his younger brother.

"NOOO! JIMMY!!!" Dobbs cried as he heard the scream of his wife.

Jimmy pushed Dobbs down the stairs. The Irishman caught his head hard on the bannister and fell, unconscious like a rag doll to the bottom of the stairs, his limp body strewn across the wooden floor.

Lorna was all alone now with no one to hear her pitiful, defenceless screams.

Chapter Forty One

Jones powered the German built car out of the city centre. He had already been to the brothers flat to find that nobody was home. It did not stop him kicking in the door and have a cursory look about. But when that proved fruitless, Jones left. Dobbs' place was on the outskirts and hopefully would be easy to find.

The suburban landscape abruptly turned into countryside. Bristol was one of those types of city. Take one road and you would be on the busy motorway, but take another and you were in a narrow country lane with only the rumbling sound of distant traffic indicating the presence of the bustling urban giant nearby.

Still dressed in the work clothes that he had visited Rachel in, Jones thought it might look odd if he was seen looking like a labourer but driving an expensive car but thought it would appear stranger if he was to attempt to change his clothes somewhere on route. He would have to stay as he was for now, even though the sleeves of the hoodie were damp from where he had held Rachel in the water. He was self-employed. He had no dress code. There was nobody assessing his work, but by his standards he was starting to get sloppy.

As he rounded the bend just before Dobbs' country home, Jones spotted a beaten up white Transit van. Through his research, he already knew what vehicle the Kinsellas used and guessed he had just got lucky.

His mobile phone vibrated from the passenger seat. The number was withheld.

"Yes." Jones answered swiftly and hoped that his need for haste was understood over the line.

"Dobbs is not to be hurt or his wife. Do not kill the Kinsellas on site if you can help it. Understood?" The voice had urgency.

"Understood!" He did not wait for the line to go dead before hanging up.

He reached into the glove compartment and pulled out a fresh pair of latex gloves, his Glock and a balaclava. Ditching the baseball cap, he replaced it with the balaclava and left the car.

The approach was silent as he neared the van, whilst pulling on the thin membrane gloves, a glance in the door mirror revealed the cab as empty. He could not hear anything from inside so assumed it to be empty.

He edged his way toward the house along the hedgerow that separated the house from the road. From the entrance of the driveway, Jones could see the whole front area of the house.

The soldier in him took over as he advanced on the house. His handgun was pointed forward from mid chest and not toward the ground as you see in televisions shows. Swift eyes took in details and disregarded those that mattered not. There was a Land rover Discovery parked on the drive, the tailgate was open showing hastily packed luggage thrown into the boot.

Jones reached the corner of the house as a woman's scream could be heard deep within the rustic styled house.

He ran to the door, which had been smashed in, the frame splintered where the lock would be. A quick glance into the hallway before a last look around outside revealed the body of a man lying face down and unconscious at the foot of the stairs, a thin bead of blood trickling from behind his ear.

Jones carefully walked into the hallway and kept his back to the wall, he could hear crying and a struggle from somewhere upstairs. He moved toward the stairs and stepped over the unmoving body which he presumed was Dobbs, the rise and fall of his ribcage showed he was still alive.

There was the sound of a slap; the back of a hand against flesh and the wretched yelp that followed. On his toes, Jones quickly climbed the stairs, careful not to make a sound but the body below and the mental image of what could be happening above created a deep sense of urgency. He might be a ruthless bastard to those he was paid to kill but sexual violence was something he detested.

As he turned the bend in the stairs, he could see the door lying in the middle of the far bedroom floor. The sounds of struggle came from the same room.

Step by step he eased his way toward the room, the military training took over he watched to see where his shadow fell as not to alert those from within the room. 'Enter swiftly. Check your corners.'

He launched himself into the room keeping his back to the wall. The scene before him was a pathetic one.

"Get off her." Jones said in a low voice. The Glock pointed toward Billy's head.

He said nothing, Billy merely climbed off the near hysterical woman and raised his hands. His flaccid penis had clearly not been able to carry out the task he was desperate to commit. The condom fell off as he stood up.

"Where's your brother?" Jones took his left hand off the handgun and reached down for the discarded dressing gown, throwing it to Lorna.

Billy shrugged his shoulders and shook his head; his face was red from failed effort and embarrassment.

"Put that away and pull your pants up," he gestured toward the now timid brothers groin area, "and you, get some clothes on" to a slightly less frightened Lorna.

Jones had to think quickly, he had four people that he needed to try and control, and the most dangerous of the crowd was nowhere to be seen.

"Call your brother upstairs but don't let him know I'm here. You got that." Jones backed into the opposite corner so he could not be seen from the door.

"J-jimmy! Jimmy, come up here." Billy shouted as he fastened his trousers.

There were sounds of movement from downstairs.

"Have you finished already?" The gruff voice of Jimmy came from the lower floor but he could be heard moving toward the staircase. "I told you I don't want to fuck her after you've had a go and Phil is stirring so get a move on." The voice grew ever closer as each heavy footstep could be heard.

Jimmy walked into the room and his mouth barely stopped moving as he noticed the intruder.

"Who the fuck are you?" Jimmy said defiantly.

"I'm the reason you are here Jimmy..." Jones was starting to tell the story but was unexpectedly interrupted.

"Are you the cunt that topped Duncs?" Jimmy cut in.

"And I'll be the cunt that tops you if you interrupt me again." Jones was not impressed, he raised his voice as he raised the gun higher to make its presence felt.

"You're gonna kill us anyway so what's the fucking difference...." Jimmy's words were abruptly halted. The sound of the unsilenced gun rang out but the shockwave from the bullet crossing the room was felt by all, but mostly by Billy as the hollow pointed round shattered his kneecap. Billy dropped to the floor screeching like a banshee.

"DO I HAVE YOUR ATTENTION NOW?" Jones screamed at the elder brother. "Right, Mrs Dobbs, please get some towels or this squealing mother fucker is going to bleed all over your nice cream carpets. Don't try anything as I will be watching you."

Lorna, now dressing in a pair of jeans and a loose blue top moved passed the standing brother and out toward the bathroom. Jones adjusted his position in the room to follow her path.

"What do you want?" Jimmy asked. He still had the arrogant manner to his voice even with his brother whimpering at his feet.

Billy gripped his wounded knee as the blood escaped between his fingers.

"I want the shotgun and the laptop."

"Well, you're shit out of luck ain't you!" Jimmy replied.

"You'll be out of luck and out of brothers if you don't tell me where they are."

"You like repeating what I say don't you? You're not the sharpest knife in the box are you?" Jimmy pushed him some more.

"Smarter than a cousin brother! So where are they?" Jones was edging up the anger scale again. His concentration was broken when Lorna came into the room and dropped the towels on the Billy but would not do anything to help him.

"We came for them too but as you can see, I ain't got them so they ain't here."

Jones swung his arm in a wide arc and pistol whipped Jimmy. Jimmy fell back but not down. Lorna screamed at the surprise strike and her yell distracted Jones for a second. A second was all Jimmy needed. He grabbed one of the towels from the floor as he stooped to recover from the hit and threw it straight into the face of the hit man.

Jones fired off a round to where he thought Jimmy was but obviously missed as Kinsella launched himself at the man. The two struggled to control the gun, Jones keeping a tight grip whilst Jimmy forced the firearm into the air. Jones swung his arm down and the butt of the gun hit Jimmy on the back of the skull, dazing him but not stopping the attack. The two men bounced off the built in wardrobes, breaking a door and a mirror as the fight intensified.

Jimmy punched the hit man in the solar plexus and took the wind out of his attacker but equally Jones was not that easily halted. The two were evenly matched but one would prevail soon enough.

Jones smashed the corner of his head into Jimmy's nose and the bigger man dropped to his knees but still held firm on the other man's wrists, using his lower position to his advantage pulling the hit man down.

Suddenly the gun went off again, Jimmy let go, instantly thinking he had been shot but he felt no pain and could see no blood. His eyes flicked across to his brother who now lay prone on the bedroom floor with a second bullet wound in his shoulder.

"YOU FUCKER!!" Jimmy screamed but he did not scream for long as the gun struck him in the face again, this time having the desired effect and stunning him to the ground.

Jones noticed what looked like a receipt hanging from Jimmy's back pocket. Without thinking he took it and hoped it important.

Out of breath and sweating, Jones tried to adjust to the situation but he was suddenly aware that Dobbs wife was no longer in the room.

From outside he heard a door slam and an engine start. He ran from the room and leapt the stairs in a single bound but he was still not quick enough, as he left through the front door the Land rover disappeared out on to the road. It had not occurred to him that Dobbs was no longer lying unconscious at the bottom of the stairs when he made the leap. The dilemma; find out what the brothers know or give chase to the Dobbs.

Jones ran to his car but the Land rover was long gone by the time he got there. If the brothers did not have the items then clearly Dobbs knew where they were, possibly hidden within the car. He climbed into the car and drove off he could not take the chance that the gunshots were not heard. Maybe this job was too much. He would have to make that phone call he did not want to make.

Chapter Forty Two

The journey flew by. David and Molly were so engrossed in each other's life story that the miles seemed effortless. Occasionally David would point out a landmark to Molly or maybe a place where he had a funny story, often involving Tom.

It was a beautiful day with beautiful company. Nothing was going to lower David's mood today. The tragic events of the past week or so and the antics of Rachel were pushed to the back of his mind. During the course of their conversation, the pair had touched on the subject of David's father. David was very candid about the fact that his father was not a factor in thirty seven of his almost forty years and although he felt a sense of loss, he was not distraught. That was David all over. He was pragmatic and a realist. He had not had a father for most of his life, then no sooner as he had established a relationship over a couple of years and half a dozen meetings, a roof top fall had brought him back to square one. It had been great while it lasted but nothing could change what had happened and David was not going to let mock grief for a man he barely knew effect his life more than it had too.

Initially, he had been broken by the news. He wanted a father. He wanted somebody to call his 'Old Man' the way his friends did. But it was not to be and David had settled back into how his life was beforehand quite easily, more easily than he thought. Maybe in a few days, weeks or months the gravity of it all would hit him but until that time came, he would carry on with his life and hopefully make Molly a permanent fixture. Only time would tell.

The journey was nearly over as Molly's purple Ford Fiesta climbed the final hill at the town limits of Milford Haven. During the course of their conversation, Molly had admitted that she had only been to Wales twice before. Once to Cardiff to see a play at the New Theatre and the other time to a wedding in a small valley town, whose name she could not remember as she could not pronounce it at the time. Her expectations for the town were of a small quaint fishing village near the sea with a handful of pubs that had old fishermen telling tall tales of their life on the open seas. The reality was much different.

Milford Haven was just the name of the waterway three hundred years previously. Originally, just a collection of small parishes and hamlets, that perched at the edge of the Welsh peninsula, fending for themselves without the badge of being a town. That all changed in the late 18th century when the potential for the large natural harbour was exploited and an American Whaling community were invited to the town for the purpose of establishing the now named Milford Haven town as a major seaport. Whaling eventually gave way to fishing as the main industry of the town until the mid/late twentieth century, when the oil companies discovered the unusually deep natural harbour could easily accommodate their massive ocean going tankers. For fifty years the area that surrounded the Haven enjoyed the affluence that the rich petrochemical companies provided but even that would end. In early 2015, there was only one oil refinery still fully operational. Two of the other sites previously used by large American oil companies were now used for the transport of liquefied natural gas but with a significantly diminished workforce. The withdrawal of these businesses and the fishing industry dwindling to just a handful of regular boats, left the large town in limbo with one generation wishing for the glory days to return and another waiting to see what the next rebirth for the town would be. Those that had not moved away to find other work stayed in the town they knew and loved and made the best of whatever employment they could find or invest their time into personal enterprise. To many, the town felt like it was teetering on the knife edge between collapse and rejuvenation.

David instructed Molly through the main road that snaked passed the suburbs to the town centre. The difference between the old and new was obvious. The newer winding roads gave way to the straight box grid design of the old town which gave it the appearance of an American town or city with parallel roads crossing other parallel roads.

Molly was taken aback at the beauty of the town. The small public gardens that sat on the corner of the road opposite the town hall were in full bloom; flowers and trees creating a little sanctuary for all to enjoy. And once on Hamilton Terrace, or Front Street as the locals called it, the town cascaded down to the river Cleddau which was the waterway of Milford Haven. There were no buildings on the left hand side of the road and this afforded an uninterrupted view of the Haven itself. Many visitors must have come to the town and looked upon the vista with widened eyes. The waterway had its own appeal to those that lived on it or near it, but there was no scene greater that gazing over the large body of water on a clear day at sunset. David hoped that he could show Molly what he loved best about the town he now called home.

They continued down the Terrace toward the Marina where David lived. The right hand side of the road was filled with large impressive buildings that the founding fathers of the town no doubt lived in. David was quick to comment on each building he had an attachment to. He pointed out the Starboard Hotel which he and Tom would frequent for a game of pool and maybe shoot the breeze with Andy the landlord before staggering back down on to the marina. Also, there was the Lord Nelson Hotel where they often had Sunday lunch, a meal that would take them into an evening of boozing followed by a DVD and maybe a few cans.

The final turn took the little car on to the Marina. Molly again was unprepared for what she thought might be a few boats, a couple of boutiques and a café. But instead she was met with dozens of yachts and cruisers in neat rows, attached to pontoons within the enclosed docks. A hundred years ago it would have been filled with fishing boats. Several modern buildings encroached on to the surrounding walkways with cafes, boutiques and letting agents on ground level with studio style apartments above, giving the already modern town a very new feel to it. Every now and then a glimpse of the past could be seen in the large corroded boats rings that edged the dock walls and the oversized discarded anchors placed in a sense of deliberate randomness.

David pointed to an empty parking space between two of the buildings and told Molly to park there. Once the car stopped there was a comfortable silence between them as they sat looking at the variety of boats before them.

Molly leaned forward and kissed him on the lips.

> "I enjoyed the journey."
>
> "So did I," he replied.
>
> "I want to see as much of your world as I can." There

was a hint of sadness in those large blue eyes.

He said nothing. He leaned into her and placed a kiss upon her lips. She responded. They were oblivious to the passers-by. For a few minutes the events of the past few days were gone, a brief respite at a stressful time, a time that would not end anytime soon. They did not know it yet, but the events of the city were chasing them down, silently; stealthily.

Chapter Forty Three

"This hurts, Jimmy. Make it stop," Billy's face was milky white and sweaty.

Jimmy had tied a tourniquet around his brother's leg and managed to stop the flow of blood from that injury but the gunshot wound to the shoulder was proving difficult to stem. With a ripped up towel stuffed into both sides of the wound, Jimmy bound the area in gaffer tape. Billy was slugging on a bottle of vodka that had been found in the kitchen.

"That's gonna have to do for now 'til we can get you fixed." Jimmy said once he had managed to seal up the hole in his brothers left shoulder.

The last twenty minutes or so had been the scariest of Jimmy's life. He felt sure that his brother was going to die in his arms. Dead at the hands of a hitman, in a house they had broken in to. The scenario did not look good from any angle but Jimmy had managed to stay calm for once and think about what he was doing. He saved his brother without screaming, punching or breaking something.

"Are you gonna take me to hospital, Jimmy?"

Jimmy knew that's what he should do but in the back of his head the same phrase kept repeating in his head, 'It's your time to shine' and that is what he had to do. To get them out of this mess and show the powers that be that he was useful to them. Whoever they were, he was going to impress them.

"Not yet Billy, it's not as bad as you think. Just flesh wounds." Jimmy lied. Even with no medical training, he could tell that his brother had a broken collar bone and a shattered kneecap. With the obvious blood loss as well, Billy was not in a good way. Jimmy placed his jacket over his brother's shoulders to cover the blood soaked shirt in preparation to leave the house.

With a broom as a makeshift crutch for Billy to use, Jimmy helped his brother down the stairs and out of the house. Somewhere in the back of his mind, he thought that there would be armed police waiting for them on the driveway, but there was nothing. The house was isolated enough that there was no one to hear the gunshots, even though the suburbs where no more than a couple of minute drive away, the events at the house went unnoticed.

As they struggled their way to the van, Jimmy could see some blood dripping from the bandaged leg and quickly ushered the injured sibling to the rear of the vehicle. Jimmy opened the doors and Billy literally fell into the dirty payload area of the vehicle.

There was an old mattress propped up at the side of the van and a couple of shabby duvets. The brothers had spent many a night sleeping in the back of the vehicle if they were on a paid labouring job. The van was cheaper than a hotel if they were working miles away.

Jimmy laid down the mattress and rolled his brother onto it. Carefully, almost paternally, he laid both the duvets over Billy and tucked him in.

For the first time ever, Jimmy felt fearful that this might be the pile of trouble they would not escape from. If Bailey had still been alive, Jimmy would have gone there first. He was now alone and would have to make the best he could of the situation. He knew that he would impress the unseen bosses if he retrieved the shotgun, regardless of whether he knew its importance or not. People were dying for it so he had to get it, whatever the cost.

Chapter Forty Four

The afternoon was a delight. It was a perfect blend of enjoyable banter, deep meaningful conversation and the occasional embrace that evolved into passionate exchanges, but that is all they were. David was trying to play it cool but it was too obvious to ignore that Molly was into him more than he had anticipated. She gazed at him with those large doe eyes and the child like giggle in her voice skipped off her tongue with each word she uttered. There was so much more to this girl that David could not fathom.

"So how well did you know my father?" It was a loaded question but he had to ask it.

"Pretty well, all my life really. He's my godfather and everything."

"Was!" David felt a pang of discomfort in correcting her on using the present tense.

"Sorry. I can't get use to the fact he's gone. I just keep thinking he'll walk back in the door again one day." Her voice had dropped an octave from the light giggly voice to a more serious tone.

"No I'm sorry. I can't put myself in a place to grieve a man I barely knew. You must be more upset than me."

"I miss him but we can't change the fact that he has gone. He was a good man and not the man you think he was. You will learn so much about him from me and my parents, and trust me he was a well-liked man. You are a lot like him in all the best ways." There was wisdom beyond her years.

"How? You barely know me." It was the first doubt he had cast over their connection.

"Your dad and Rachel talked about you a lot. Rachel was soft on you. You may have picked up on that?" She paused for an answer.

"I didn't get that." He lied and put the early morning incident to the back of his mind once more.

"Well she was but she was soft on lots of people. I don't know how your dad put up with her. She was so easily led astray." There was a bitter taste in her words.

"Did she cheat?"

"Often."

"Why didn't he leave her?" David asked.

"I think he felt responsible for her. He'd saved her from herself. I know that her home life as a kid wasn't the best and she had no real family to help her or guide her." Molly eyes dropped to the floor, maybe for the sadness of the loss of John Hill or perhaps the unhappy childhood that shaped Rachel's personality. Either way, Molly's usually bubbly demeanour had left her briefly.

David wanted to the lift the mood back up but wanted to leave an appropriate pause between the subject that brought the atmosphere down and what he was so desperately trying to come up with. He put the kettle on and washed up the mugs that had been filled three times already that afternoon. He loved her company. More so than any woman he had ever met. She made him feel alive.

"So, meal and drinks or drinks and a Chinese? What do you want to do?" David asked trying to divert the conversation from the negative path it was heading.

"I don't mind." Her voice still echoed with distraction. "You can choose."

"Whatever we do, it will be my treat." He playfully threw a scatter cushion toward her.

Molly caught the cushion and a smile broke on her perfect face once more. She gasped in taunting disbelief and threw it back at him. The pair laughed at each other as the buoyant atmosphere returned. The hope that this would remain was deep within them both. They knew that their lives although not unhappy were somehow incomplete and their meeting felt so right for them.

"I have to buy at least one round of drinks." Molly said.

"I might allow you…" David's sentence was cut short by the intercom buzzer trilling an interruption. The pair looked at each other blankly as David walked over to the income.

"Hello?" David answered.

Silence.

"Hello? Who's there?"

The buzzer rasped into life, making David jump as he was so close to the speaker.

"It's probably Amble, from downstairs playing about." David explained to Molly.

"Who?"

Amble Goodrich was the old man from the ground floor that had adopted both Tom and David as his grandsons, so to speak. Ambrose was his real name but he had a very short shuffling gait when he walked, so had been given the name nickname Amble

"I'll tell you later." David pressed the entry button. "Come on in."

The muffled clunk of the lobby door opening and the slam that followed echoed in the hollow hallway. The mystery caller could now be heard walking up the staircase. The echo of footsteps in the enclosed staircase could be heard climbing slowly toward the top floor. Amble walked quicker for an old guy, so it definitely was not him.

Chapter Forty Five

The drive back to the flat was a cautious one. Jimmy did not want to attract any unwanted attention so he kept the van under the speed limit, making doubly sure as he approached traffic lights that the lights were in his favour. There was also the small matter of his brother lying under the duvets behind him and how carefully he could negotiate speed humps and roundabouts, not wishing to harm Billy more than he already had been.

There had been a few tense moments crossing the city when police cars came into view. One had even pulled in directly behind the battered old van at a set of lights. Jimmy had prayed for the first time in his life that all his lights and tyres were in good order so he would not get stopped. A defective brake light was one thing but explaining away the two bullet holes in his brother would be impossible to do.

Jimmy parked in the parking bays at the rear of the flats so as not to be seen from the road. He had not planned to be longer than ten minutes, grab a change of clothes for Billy and himself plus some supplies; food and painkillers mostly but Jimmy had one other thing to collect, a weapon.

Luckily, there were hardly any people out and about. Jimmy was able to get from the van to the flat without passing anyone on the stairwell or landing, which was fortunate, as Jimmy had not realised the amount of blood that covered his clothes. There were a few drops of blood on his dirt covered jeans but his long sleeved t-shirt had a significant stain across his middle which he tried to hide by folding his arms. He felt he was drawing more attention to himself but on the estate that he lived on nobody would care or dare ask something of someone with Jimmy's reputation.

He stopped dead in his tracks. The front door to the flat had been forced. The door was only ajar by an inch or so but there was a footprint on the paintwork and the wood had splintered at the lock.

Jimmy cautiously pushed the door open slowly while standing to one side of the frame; nothing. He quickly shot a glance down the hallway. There were signs of some disruption but the flat was never well kept, although Jimmy could tell that his home had been turned over before he even set foot inside.

He cursed himself for not having a weapon of any sort tucked away in his sock or in his waistband like they do in the movies, but this was not the movies, this was his flat, in the here and now. There was no sound from within. Jimmy stepped through the front door and inched his way toward the kitchen. His primary thought was to get a weapon and search the other rooms but in the back of his mind was the image of Billy bleeding out in the back of the van.

As he passed the open door to the small lounge, Jimmy could see the room had been tossed. What were they looking for? He had nothing of any value nor did Billy. Every penny they raised through legitimate or illegitimate means was spent on their chaotic, drinking and smoking lifestyle. It was not unusual for the brothers to earn a grand over a week of hard graft and then blow the lot in the pub or at the bookies over the course of a weekend. Those times had to change; time to shine.

He entered the ransacked kitchen. Cutlery, tools and unopened mail was scattered across the floor. All the drawers had been tipped out and thrown in the corner of the room.

Jimmy picked up a large kitchen knife and moved towards the bedrooms. Both had been turned over but there was no sign of the house breaker. If the events of the last few days had not been weird enough already but this had just pushed the bizarre needle right off the chart. They had nothing of value. Why break in?

Then it dawned on him that it must have been the mystery man with the gun at Dobbs' house that had called earlier. A horrific thought entered his mind. If they had been at home when the gunman called then they might have been dead by now. Jimmy could not see a man like that calling for the merchandise and saying 'farewell and thanks for goods'. No, he and Billy would have been shot execution style through the forehead like Flynn had. This was a game changer and Jimmy needed to change how he played.

He dashed back into his bedroom and to the bottom of his wardrobe. The only clothes that he ever hung up were a few shirts and his suit but even these had been thrown onto the bed, leaving the flimsy wardrobe looking rather forlorn and empty, with one of the doors hanging off at the top hinge.

Jimmy prised off the front panel at the base and reached his large hand under. He grabbed what he had come for and pulled out a dirty cloth sack. He tipped out the contents of the sack onto the floor. The smell of gun oil was very pungent. Lying on the carpet was an old automatic pistol, a Second World War Browning 9mm. Also, a half dozen loose bullets and a bundle of money, two hundred pounds in a mix of tens and fives.

Quickly, Jimmy changed into some cleaner clothes and stuffed the money into his pocket. The pistol was loaded and slipped into the front of his waistband. He grabbed some of Billy's sportswear, a packet of painkillers and a bottle of vodka; all were shoved into a grimy rucksack. With the rucksack over his shoulder, Jimmy ducked out of the flat hopefully, for the last time. He was a gambling man and he hoped he would not lose big this time, because this time he was gambling with far more than his ill gotten money.

Chapter Forty Six

There was a subtle tapping at the door. David gripped the lock but did not turn it. He looked through the spyhole but there was nothing to see as the lens had been covered by whoever was outside.

"Who's there?" David asked.

More light knocking against the wood of the door. Molly looked pensive.

"Don't open it!" She said.

He threw her a bemused glance but opened the door anyway. David was greeted with the sight of Tom, a case of beer tucked under one arm, a bottle of wine and a bag of Chinese food in his free hand and another bag of food gripped in his mouth. David took the bag that was between Tom's teeth.

"Jeez! What kept you?" The out of breath Tom asked as he stumbled through the door.

"I don't know who it was." David replied.

"It's hard to talk with a chicken chow mein and a bag of chips hanging out of your gob you know!" Tom said as he dropped the rest of the goods onto the kitchen counter.

"What are you doing here?"

"David, it's a Friday night. It's beer and Chinese night. I've even brought enough for the young lady." Tom said holding up the bottle of Rose he had thoughtfully bought for Molly.

"I thought we might skip it tonight with..well, you know?" David gestured toward the new female addition to the flat.

Tom spotted dead in his tracks. He glanced at David, then at Molly and then at the food and drink.

"Oh! Okay!" Tom quickly emptied the bags of food on the counter and then packed one with the food he had purposely brought for himself. "It's alright. I know when I'm not wanted." He then filled one of the empty food bags with half a dozen cans of beer and made for the door.

"Look you don't have to go." David felt bad for his friend.

"It's ok I'll go downstairs and bother Amble." Tom pulled open the door and stepped into the hallway. He turned back to David, who had a slightly dejected look on his face. "Keep it down the pair of you if you don't mind." Tom winked and made his way back down the stairwell.

David shut the door and laughed.

"Does he always do that?" Molly asked smiling from the sofa.

"Too many times," David smiled broadly as he delved into the food to see what delights his friend had left for them.

The earlier question of food had been answered but it was just the rest of the evening that had to be figured out.

Jones had stopped just outside on the main marina road. He could see a figure of a man walk out of the top floor flat through the large window that extended from the lobby all the way up the corner of the building. He watched the man walk to the ground floor and knock on the door of the ground level flat. Within a few second the door opened and the man disappeared inside.

Jones was sure that it looked like the man who had escorted John Hill's grieving partner out of the hotel when she was very drunk and emotional. Clearly the address on the receipt had been correct.

There was no point in doing anything tonight. The parcel would not arrive to until the next day. Jones pulled away to find a place to sleep the night. Tomorrow he would return.

Chapter Forty Seven

Within an hour of leaving the ransacked flat Jimmy had managed to buy some medical supplies to patch up Billy and then hit the road. He had bought some antiseptic liquid, gauze and bandages then set to work on redressing his brother's wounds. Jimmy had surprised himself at how well the emergency bandages, made from ripped towels, had worked. The wounds although still weeping, had stopped flowing with blood and the injured brother seemed somehow brighter, but that could have been because of the mixture of painkillers washed down with vodka.

Still being cautious with the driving, Jimmy headed straight for the motorway. He figured that with Dobbs couriering the shotgun to John Hill's son and it not likely to arrive until tomorrow at the earliest, that way he would have time to get to the town then find the address. He wished he had remembered the full address but at least he knew the town. How big could a Welsh town be he thought?

Carefully reaching back, he pulled the pistol from the back of his waistband. The heavy weapon felt uncomfortable tucked into his jeans, so he dropped it into the deep door pocket of the van and covered it with a scrunched up bundle of blue tissue paper, the kind that is always found on service station forecourts. The gun was essential. He was about to step into the big boys league. The big boys used big toys. Jimmy had one of his own now and would use it if he had to.

Violence was an ever present factor in the Kinsellas existence since they were very young. The legacy of their unstable upbringing had dulled the trauma that violence generally brought with it. Both brothers had broken bones and permanent scars from the endless conflicts that had befallen them over the years. Some kind of clash was always around the corner. Jimmy often reverted to using his fists before opening his mouth but he knew he had to be smarter from now on.

Could he kill? Most definitely! Who was he going to kill? He would start with the man who shot his brother first. It would not be the first time Jimmy had killed a man. To his brother it would be but not to Jimmy. He had a deep dark secret that he had kept from his brother all these years.

There were always rumours about who did what to whom, who killed who and what happened to those that were never heard of again. The criminal rumour mill exaggerated its own crimes but this was one that Jimmy had always denied even though he was the most likely to have committed it, and that was the murder of his father.

Jimmy was only twenty at the time and looked like the younger version of his father. He was tall, lean and powerfully built. His steel blue eyes had a harsh wisdom about them, yet his skin was young and taut. The obvious difference between the two men was their outlook on life.

James was a happy-go-lucky kind of guy, a loveable rogue at best and an opportunist at worst. He had sailed through his life with little regard for the responsibilities he had created along the way. Every penny he earned or stole funded his chaotic, drink fuelled, woman chasing lifestyle. He was a petty criminal pursuing a hedonistic dream. Responsibility was for others, not him.

Jimmy had just crept out of his teens and had faced more life changing situations and been far more accountable to those that touched his life on a daily basis. For all the bad that had happened to him, he still felt the need to try and please the people that counted, including the almost childlike Billy. It would take another two decades before he had to face the reality that it was only his younger brother that appreciated his efforts.

After a chance meeting in a pub, father and son tried to establish some form of bond. Although the bonding effort was all one way, with James not really committing to his eldest son and not wanting any acknowledgement from Billy. The disappointment felt within Jimmy was deeply personal. They had a few meetings, but James was always looking for the door unless there was a drink in front of him. Jimmy started festering resentment toward his estranged father and slowly distanced himself from the man.

One day, out of the blue, James contacted Jimmy and asked to meet him down at a disused warehouse on the far side of the Bristol Docks. Jimmy arrived an hour early to find this father already waiting for him, covered in cuts and bruises. James had obviously taken a beating from somebody with a beef.

"What happened to you?" Jimmy asked. He anticipated that his father's desire to see him was nothing to do with parental culpability.

"You know me son, taking one chance too many."

The word 'Son' had no relevance to this conversation. Jimmy knew that he was there as a last chance bail out for his father.

"What do you want from me?" The tone did not reveal Jimmy's inner rage.

"Just a few quid to keep them off my back" James said pitifully, the buoyancy that usually infected his voice was completely absent. "I was wondering if you could help your old man out."

"How much?"

"It's for a bookie son, I made a few bets and they.."

"How much?" Jimmy's voice was louder than the first time of asking.

"Well...I borrowed some from..." James stalled.

"How much? What's the total?" Rage had now spilled into the words.

James shuffled awkwardly, despite him approaching sixty he acted like a guilty teenager, caught out by an adult who made them feel like a child.

"There's two mon..." James did not finish the sentence.

"HOW FUCKING MUCH??" The scream echoed around the empty warehouse.

"Two grand!" He spat out.

A hostile silence swelled within the shell of the building. Jimmy internalized twenty years of let-down and dissatisfaction to the point of explosion. The next word out of his mouth followed the inevitable punch that bloodied the nose of his already battered father.

"YOU! USELESS! FUCK!" Each word was punctuated with a punch or a kick. The initial blow had dropped his father to the ground and left him vulnerable. The rest of the attack was carried out in silence. The dull thuds reverberating off the rusted corrugated roof were the only sound.

There was no response. No arms raised in defence. No pleas for mercy.

Breathless, Jimmy stood over the pulverised body and felt no loss. The last moment of emotion he was ever consumed by for his father was shown in an outburst of rage. A rage that now flowed like a tap that could never be turned off. With the adrenalin seeping into his trembling limbs, Jimmy walked away; never looking back. That chapter was now closed forever.

In the present day, with the steering wheel pinched between his large battered fingers, Jimmy felt the flow of that rage coursing through his veins once more. He would seek revenge on the man who had shot his brother. After he had retrieved the items and secured a better future for himself and his brother, he would find the man and kill him; slowly and methodically.

Chapter Forty Eight

The food went down well, too well, as did the drink. Instead of slipping out to one of nearby pubs for further drinks, David decided to take Molly for a walk to show her some of his adopted home town and to ease off some of the fullness from their stomachs.

The steep hill from the marina up to the crest of Hamilton Terrace caused Molly's thighs to burn from lactic acid build up. David laughed at her struggling like an invalid. He liked to run on his days off to keep himself fit and he would always run the hill first. He and Tom had contemplated maybe an epic trip to climb Kilimanjaro or something like that. The friends had thought that Milford Haven would be the ideal training ground because of all its hills. The locals were used to the gradients but the young woman from Bristol was not. She only climbed a hill if she was out on the town, and then had alcohol to ease her pain to the top of Park Street in the centre of Bristol.

The long, arrow straight Hamilton Terrace looked beautiful in the orange glow of the setting sun. As it slowly descended, just hovering above the rooftops on the west side of the town, it cast long dark shadows that seemed to have no end. A silent breeze cooled the warmth that still resided in the comfortable air of that summer evening. They walked silently along the marina side of the street their hands subconsciously finding each other. Strolling like a couple that had walked together many times before and not as two people on the cusp of a new relationship, they took in the views of the haven while the rest of the world slid by. Each and every moment was a joy.

As they reached the junction for The Rath, the street with best possible views of the haven, the pair paused and gazed down the full length of the estuary. The deep waters rippled a mirror image of the deep orange and purple sky left by the vacating sun. It had now completely dropped from view, creating a featureless silhouette on the far side of town. David stood behind Molly and wrapped his arms around her, resting his head on her shoulder so that their cheeks touched. She nestled back into him and he could feel her relax against his body; a beautiful scene with a beautiful woman, a perfect moment on a perfect day. They held that timeless moment as one.

Street lights started to come on as the night was drawing in. The lights on the jetties on both sides of the haven had already come on, bringing an artificial beauty to the scene. With each passing minute the heat of the day started to dissipate, David feeling Molly shiver against his warm body as the chill took over. It was time to go.

The pair walked down the steep slip hill toward the beach. It was not a beach covered in sand but covered in red limestone pebbles of various sizes; some small enough to almost be considered sand, some the size of house bricks. David did not take Molly on to the beach but along the path back toward the flat. The air was colder still as they neared the water but Molly still wanted to look at the marina.

The masts of all the yachts and cruisers, jet black in the twilight, splintered the now purple sky. They could have been anywhere in the world at that moment. There was nothing to indicate a country or a province, just boats and water. The lapping of the water against the many hulls and the clicking of the rigging lines tapping against the masts was interrupted by the occasional cheer or laugh from the elevated out door eating areas of the marinas restaurants and bars.

"Do you want to go for a drink?" David asked. He really did not want to go for a drink but with the bars so close he felt obliged to ask.

"Just one, just so we can say we've been out for a drink." She smiled that wide smile.

"Okay! But I'm buying."

"If you insist kind Sir,"

"I do, I do."

The pair laughed as they linked arms and climbed the steps up to the external mezzanine where they would actually have several drinks huddled under a patio heater before staggering back to the flat close to midnight, happy in each other's company. Unaware of what the next day would bring.

Jimmy took a big swig from the vodka bottle. He watched Molly and John Hill's son walk through the lobby door of the apartment block. He could only imagine what the pair would get up to once in the privacy of the flat. Jealousy burned through his veins to settle in the pit of his stomach. He drowned the feeling with another slug of vodka.

Settling down under the duvet next to his brother, Jimmy did not want to think any more about what could be happening in the building ahead of him. He had too much floating around in his head as it was. There was no time to think of the 'what' and the 'why'. He needed to focus on the goal. Nothing or no one was getting in his way now, man, woman or contract killer; no one at all.

Chapter Forty Nine

The morning sun forced its way between the slats of the Velux blind to illuminate the room. David awoke and stared at the open blinds that he had forgotten to close in his anticipation of how the night would end.

To his left was a sleeping Molly. The warmth of her skin brushed against his as she stirred.

They touched, kissed and held each other until sleep took over the comfortable consciousness they shared. In a way David was more than happy their relationship had not taken that next step just yet. There was no need to rush, no need at all.

He looked down upon her perfect face, thinking it almost too perfect. It was as if she had been drawn by an artist who had only seen beauty in their lifetime. Molly's eyes still looked large and childlike even while she slept. David was sure that all the beautiful heroines from the Japanese Manga cartoons must be have been based on her features.

Molly eyes flickered open and caught David looking at her.

"Morning" he said not minding being caught out.

"Morning you" she replied. Her eyes shutting again as she stretched and yawned. Even that was perfect.

"Did you sleep well?"

"Like a log, you?"

"Your snoring kept me awake all night" David laughed as he said it.

Her reaction was to punch him playfully on the arm and climb on top of him, trying to pin him to the bed. They struggled and laughed briefly as David tickled her waist as she straddled him. Her small but perfectly formed breasts jiggled within the thin lace bra that barely covered them.

As the play fight intensified one of her breasts freed itself from the material. This stopped the fooling around as David was mortified. He thought she may be offended. He did not know why, but she might have been, he still did not know her at all.

"I'm so, so sorry" he said trying to hide his embarrassment.

"It's okay," she laughed at his awkwardness. Her hands moved behind her back and unhooked the offending piece of lingerie. "Oops!" She discarded the item and looked deep into his eyes.

There was recognition in the pause that followed. They both knew what would come next.

Molly leaned forward and kissed him passionately, her tongue flickering against his as he wrapped his arms around her, pinning her slender frame on top of him. Her hands gripped his face as she kissed him harder, trying to force herself almost into his mouth.

Their bodies writhed together as hands wandered and touched, exploring new ground and enjoying what was found. David's hand slid down her back and inside the back of her thin panties, his fingers tightly gripped her buttock. He felt her grind herself against him. The excitement built swiftly between them. She took his free hand and put it on her breast. Her hand returned to his head, long elegant fingers entwined with his hair and tugged at his scalp. They were lost to the moment. The remaining clothing that separated them was soon removed and with that final barrier gone there was only one last step to take.

The love making was unhurried and unpressured. Their union was seamless, perfect, wonderful and beyond expectation.

Chapter Fifty

Jones parked up in the herringbone parking bays of the next block of flats over. It had not escaped his attention that the Kinsellas dirty white Transit van was parked directly outside the lobby door of the correct block. 'Thick as a sack of rocks' sailed through his mind, although he could not believe that Jimmy Kinsella had managed to come all this way without the address.

Maybe he had underestimated the intelligence or the tenacity of a small time thug trying to elevate himself up the criminal league table. Clearly there was some kind of ambition that the elder brother was aspiring to. Jones had encountered that kind of ambition before. It made people dangerous.

But what of the younger brother, he thought. Jones knew that Billy had two bullets in him, not in necessarily vital areas but any gunshot wound could kill, even in a limb. The rounds in his Glock had a full metal jacket and had probably passed completely through the flesh of Billy, regardless of how thick set he was. Whatever the situation, he only had one brother to contend with. Possibly, Jimmy had done the right thing and dropped his injured brother at a hospital anonymously. If he had not then Billy was now a liability and likely to slow Jimmy down.

In a way, Jones hoped for the former, it would mean only one body to dispose of in a part of the country where his knowledge was limited.

Jones took a swig of his coffee purchased from a Drive-Thru on his way from a local hotel. He was always careful to wear a baseball cap in such situations so CCTV would not capture his image. It did not matter about the license plates of his car as they were fakes and would be changed the next day for other fake plates. He was prepared, as always, for any eventuality; 9mm pistol in the glove compartment, the magazine filled with hollow points for a single shot kill, and a knife tucked into his sock. Prepared, like a boy scout. The rest was just a waiting game. Today he would wait for a very long time.

Chapter Fifty One

Tom was roused from a sweet dream about the new barmaid of The Starboard by a firm hand pounding on his front door. A quick glance at his alarm clock told him he had slept later than normal. The red diodes blinked 9:28.

He had dragged himself home from Amble Goodrich's flat at 2ish in the morning. He and David liked old Amble. They loved the old man's tales of life on the open sea with the Merchant Navy. The pair spent many a night drinking into the early hours listening eagerly.

The rapping at the door continued as Tom pulled on a shabby pair of joggers and hurried down the stairs of the house. He could make out a large form through the two frosted glass front doors. He was not expecting anybody at this time of the morning and the figure was too tall to be David.

As he opened the inner door he could make out a large man with a cap on his head. He could not remember ordering anything online recently. The figure could be seen turning toward the door in response to hearing the catch of the inner door.

Tom unlocked the front door, confused by the intrusion into his morning of peaceful slumber. The door was barely open when the man thrusted a package into Tom's hands.

"Could I get a signature pal?" The courier followed up by holding a PDA and a plastic stylus.

"Yeah" was all Tom could manage as the morning sun blinded his tired eyes. He took the PDA and scribbled a virtual signature across the screen.

"What's the surname?" The huge man asked.

Tom glanced at the name on the package. The name on the top stated 'Mr D Hill' so he went with that.

"Hill!" he said almost as a question rather than a statement as it was not his surname.

"Cheers pal." The man turned away and headed for his van.

Tom stood in the open doorway for a moment taking in the view. He lived above the Marina and could see pretty much all of it from his front door. It was a truly gorgeous day. The sky was a deep blue and cloudless. The sun shone like a ball of white light at the left side of a perfect picture opportunity. He did not have a camera, but he did have a mystery package in his hand, a cardboard box, heavily wrapped in parcel tape and measuring eighteen inches by twelve but only four inches deep. It had weight to it but was not heavy, but what was more puzzling was why the parcel for David sent to him?

Chapter Fifty Two

Four hours had clocked by and still Jones waited. There had been no sign of movement from the flat or Kinsella's van. A truck load of workmen from the local council in Hi-Vis jackets had turned up just after 8am and started marking the road for groundwork of some kind. With the amount of activity that was now happening, it was unlikely that Jones could make a move. But he was patient and being paid regardless.

He wondered if Jimmy had spotted him yet. He doubted it. The plates of the car had been changed since the incident at Dobbs' house. Black BMWs were ten a penny which was the idea, seen one, seen them all. They blended in. Plus Jones had parked a good hundred yards away. Even if he had been seen, what could Jimmy do? He was not about to confront an armed professional like Jones, or call the police for that matter. Although, if anyone did call it in, it would have to be the local Firearms Team and Jones would not go quietly. If it was a choice of a few dead cops for his liberty or holding his hands up and spend an undetermined amount of time behind bars then it was a no brainer, he would shoot his way out.

Another council vehicle turned up and parked right in front of the building blocking the view while the eager Hi-Vis brigade started to unload the equipment off the back. Jones had to make a quick choice, either stay where he was or get out of the car to gain a better vantage point. He decided to stay put and not draw attention to himself. As much as he was fearless of the law, he still wanted to complete the job, maintain his reputation and move on. Besides if a delivery was made the only road to or from the flat was still fully visible.

Tom called his friend to tell him of the mystery package. David knew nothing about it but had told him to drop it down when he was able, also to come and help himself to some breakfast. Tom would never miss out on a free meal and was out the door as soon as possible, choosing to walk instead of driving. He used the path alongside the marine to stay in the warmth of the sun.

As he turned the corner he was confronted by a half dozen local council workers unloading an open back truck. Tom negotiated his way around the workforce and let himself into the building. He was not handicapped by an arm full of beer and Chinese food this time, so he did not have to buzz in. He was oblivious to the white Transit van parked just a few metres away and could not even see the black BMW because of the council truck obscuring his view.

He climbed the stairs quickly and was greeted by David offering him a mug of coffee.

    "Now that's what I call service!" Tom said.

    "Latte with two sugars, just how you like it" David replied.

The flat smelled like a greasy spoon café with coffee and bacon being the dominant odours. Tom walked in to see the two empty plates on the counter top and a full plate just for him.

"Aw you shouldn't have." Tom picked the plate up and greedily started to tuck in after handing the package to David.

David cut the tape and prised open the box, inside was a laptop bag. Rather bemused,

David took a seat and started to unzip the bag. With that Molly entered from the bedroom.

"Is that a laptop?" she asked.

"Er...yeah" David was very confused.

She walked right up to him and placed a hand on the zip to stop him from opening it anymore. Molly leaned into him and put her lips against his ear.

"Take it with us, I know who sent it" she whispered carefully so Tom could not hear.

"Who?"

"Later. Away from here" a finger placed on her lips silenced him as she reached for her handbag. "We should go and see the beach you keep talking about" she rapidly changed the subject.

"Let me guess, Newgale?" Tom said with a mouth full of bacon. The whispered exchange had been lost on him but he heard the plan for the day.

"But of course," David said, "there's no beach better in the county. Scratch that! The country even"

"Let's go then!" Molly said with her eyes wide as if to say 'Right Now!' and gripping David's arm, willing him out of the seat.

"You're gonna leave me here?" Tom protested.

"Yeah, help yourself to the food but make sure you wash up afterwards," David said, "wash our stuff too."

Tom had one of those sad puppy dog looks on his face. He knew they wanted to be alone together but he had not figured on two days away from his best friend.

"No worries. I'll download some porn to your laptop, run up a Box Office bill on your Sky account and make some long distance phone calls while I'm here."

"Don't you dare! Dickhead!"

"I'm your dickhead brethren." Tom said. He did not even watch them go out the door. He merely picked up the TV remote and switched the set on. His head did not even turn as the door slammed shut.

"Will he be alright?" Molly said as they made their way down the stairs.

"He'll be fine. He'll eat all he can and then go and see Amble for an hour or two."

"Will he wash up?"

"I doubt it."

They laughed together as they stepped out into the morning air. The work men seemed to be just starting on whatever they were doing outside the flat. There would be some drilling and digging by the look of the equipment on show. Staying in the flat would be a noisy business today so going out was definitely the best idea.

Molly popped the locks on her little purple car but David noticed that she glanced back over her shoulder twice as they approached the car. They entered the vehicle almost simultaneously.

"What's bothering you?" David asked.

"Oh, you noticed?" She placed the keys into the ignition and started the engine without looking at him.

"Yeah,"

"Well don't look now but there's a white van parked behind us and to the left," again she did not look at him, she simply reversed the car out of the space and turned around "it belongs to the Kinsellas, the two rough looking Neanderthals that Tom pissed off at the wake."

"Really! How do you know?" David could not help but cast an eye toward the van.

"They use to park it in the yard," again she tried to look like she was ignoring everything but driving "I had to look at it every day so I know it's theirs."

The car pulled out onto the marina road and Molly obeyed the 10mph limit, more so because she did not want to appear like she was spooked. The van also pulled out from its space and followed.

"They're following." The nerves were very present in Molly's voice.

"What do you think they want?" David was calm. He did not know the Kinsellas as Molly did.

"Now is not the time. We have to lose them." Molly's breathing quickened as the nerves turned to fear.

"Ok, follow what I say and we'll lose them," David said, "this car has to be quicker than that van."

As they reached the junction that leaves the marina the car paused at the give way line. The van held back trying not to be seen but failing.

There was an arrow on the road directing all vehicles to turn left, not because the traffic was one way but because it was easier to negotiate the junction. When there was a break in the flow of cars David instructed Molly to turn right and accelerate up the hill as fast as she could then take the first left. She did as she was told.

David then took her on a path through the town which only the locals would know so well. It took just a few more turns and the Kinsellas would have no way of knowing which way the Fiesta had gone. Within a few minutes they were leaving the town via one of the small hamlets. Unless an individual was very familiar with the area it was the kind of place that remained invisible to the casual visitor.

"They are as good as lost." David said with a smirk across his face.

"Good." Molly's expression was not as smug. Her heart was still beating at twice the speed it should be.

"Hey," David placed his hand on her tightly clenched fist that gripped the gearstick, "Its ok. We lost them."

"They'll find us again if they get the chance and we might not be so lucky."

"What's the worst that can happen?" it was a question that David wished he had never asked.

Tears started to roll down her face. Her face was an image of horror.

"You don't want to know?" She struggled to get the words out.

"I do. And I want to know what the deal is with the laptop?"

"There's so much you need to know."

"About?" David asked.

She said nothing for a moment as if to compose herself. The tears had stopped for now but it seemed they could return at any minute. Her face appeared to age before him, whatever revelations she would have to declare obviously hung heavy on her slender shoulders.

David said nothing but his body language suggested he was eager to know all as he twitched and fidgeted in the passenger seat.

"Your father" she glanced across toward him as she spoke the answer with those large blue eyes showing a real sadness beyond the redness and tears that invaded them.

"What about him?"

"He was hunted by a professional hitman."

The statement impacted like a sledgehammer to the chest. Any words that were to come from his mouth would need the air that he could not breathe into his lungs. He gasped in disbelief but internally he knew there was something else to this whole situation. He knew that Rachel was more scared than grief stricken at the funeral. Maybe this was reason. Maybe she knew. There was an air of make believe surrounding his father. Whatever it was, it must have been enough to get him killed.

An eternity passed, or so it seemed and then Molly spoke.

"There is more." She said cautiously.

"Do I want to know?"

"You have to." her voice was filled with sorrow for him, "your life is in danger too."

Chapter Fifty Three

Jones had ducked down in his seat when he saw the white van driving away. He did not want Jimmy Kinsella to see him at all. It was obvious that Kinsella was following the couple in the purple Fiesta; the couple from the funeral. Jones remembered the girl; tall, slim, blonde and very pretty. He might be a professional killer but he was still a man with both a working pair of balls and eyes. That was how he saw it anyway.

He was not going anywhere yet. There was a package being delivered to the building and he was not leaving until it turned up. He had the slip in his hand which he took as proof it was coming. As it was, he did not have to wait much longer. A courier vehicle pulled up directly outside of the building.

Jones made his move and parked his car in the space where the Kinsellas' the white van had been parked. He had been quick enough to get into the space before the courier driver had managed to jump out. If he was lucky he might be able to intercept the package without anyone else getting hurt. He was not that lucky.

The courier leapt out of the small van with a long package in his hand. As he hit the buzzer, the door opened and a man came out. Jones recognised him as the man that was helping John Hill's grieving girlfriend.

"Who's that for pal?" The man said.

"Flat 5, David Hill"

Jones hung back for a minute, waiting for an appropriate moment and trying to think of an angle to get him in the door.

"I'll sign for it fella!" The man piped up.

There was a quick scribble of a signature and the package disappeared inside the building. A moment later, the courier backed out and was gone.

Jones also observed the workmen jumping into their van and driving away. He took a quick glance at his watch. It must be an early lunchtime as all the equipment had been left behind.

An opportunity had presented itself. Jones got out of the car and walked up to the door. He pressed the button marked number five with latex covered finger.

"Yeah?" a voice crackled at the other end of the intercom.

"I've got a parcel for flat five" Jones said in his best courier voice; however that was supposed to sound.

"Well you've hit the right button for that. I'll buzz you in."

"No..wait..I need a hand to carry it in. Could I get a lift in with it?"

"OK, I'll be down now." The intercom clicked off.

Jones stood by the car and opened the boot. He surveyed the road in both directions and looked for any persons nearby.

There was nobody that he could see. He hoped it would stay like that for a minute or two longer.

The door opened. The man that had greeted the courier propped the door open with a fire extinguisher and made his way out to greet the mystery caller.

"Is it big or heavy?"

"Come see for yourself," Jones glanced down into the plastic covered empty boot, trying to give the impression that there was indeed something there. He was more than certain this was the guy at the funeral and the wake. He was at the right address and he had already signed for a package in the name of David Hill. Jones must have the right guy; surely.

"You just caught me, I was abo…hey!"

As Tom reacted to the empty boot, Jones wrapped his muscular arm around the confused man's neck and pulled back hard. 'There is some fight in this one' Jones thought as he struggled to restrain the man. Tom kicked off the boot of the car and threw his head back catching Jones just above the left eye. Jones pulled his arm tighter and the held his body rigid. It only took a moment. There was a feeble attempt to prise the arm away from the throat but soon both arms fell limp. The sleeper hold had worked again.

Jones dropped the body into boot and tucked in the limbs. Cable tie cuffs and duct tape were applied as a matter of caution as he patted down the body looking for the keys to the flat. The front right-hand jeans pocket had what he was looking for. A quick scout about revealed there was still nobody nearby and he had not been seen. He slammed the boot shut and turned toward the open door behind him.

The stairs were bounded three at a time right to the top floor where flat five was situated. The front door was on the catch and only needed to be pushed open. There was nobody home.

The newly arrived package was on the kitchen counter. He swiftly grabbed it and was about to leave when, out of the corner of his eye, Jones spied another package but this one had been opened. He picked up the box. There was nothing in it apart from ripped bubble-wrap. The address on the outside was different from one on the long slender package. Different courier services had also been used. One may have nothing to do with the other but Jones needed to be thorough.

A quick recce of the flat proved fruitless. Time was of the essence and he could not afford another minute searching for the mystery item now. He had to go.

The descent of the stairs was the same as the ascent. Three steps at a time. He got to the bottom and was just about to leave the building when he heard a voice.

    "I've called the police. You won't get away with it"

Jones could make out half a face of an elderly man peering around the ground floor flat door. A security chain limited the gap between the edge of the door and the frame.

"What do you mean?" Jones asked in his calm professional voice.

"I saw what you did? Let my friend out of your ca..." the sentence was cut short.

A swift kick opened the door off the chain and the short old man tumbled back into the flat with the force. Jones stepped into the flat and reached into his waistband. The Glock was pulled, aimed, fired and back in the waistband inside of three seconds. Amble Goodrich had been shot through the forehead, execution style.

It was definitely time to go. He dropped the long thin package into the boot next to the unconscious body but he did not shut it. A swift tug at the registration plate ripped it off to reveal another plate with a different vehicle identity beneath. The same was done at the front of the car and the fake plates were also dropped next to Tom's bound and gagged body.

As he raced away from the block of flats, somewhere in the distance, Jones could hear a siren heralding the arrival of the Police the old man had called.

"Too bad they're gonna be too late" Jones uttered aloud. It would be a close call, even by his standards. Either way, he had made a mistake and been seen. There was no scope for any more mistakes.

Chapter Fifty Four

The rest of the car journey was a silent affair. David was not talking. He was nervous about what other revelations Molly may have to say.

Molly was not talking because she needed to gather her thoughts on how the rest of the story would be told. A point of a finger to indicate direction was the limit of communication from David. The last instruction came in the form of a few words.

"Pull over on the right here." He said. His voice devoid of emotion, like the gravity of the tale had stifled any feeling from escaping his lips.

Molly did as she was told. She pulled up in a very wide layby that crested the hill on the way down to the beach village of Newgale. In her eyes, David had not been wrong with his enthusiasm for the place. The vista was incredible. It was impossible to see much of the beach from where they parked but still the sight was impressive.

The canopy was a deep cloudless blue with the occasional trail from a passenger plane dispersing leisurely, yet not spoiling the near perfect scene, as the sky touched down on the horizon, meeting the water like old friends. A rugged peninsular dominated the right side of the picture. Cliffs stood firm against the crashing waves as they had done for thousands of years, the sea water slowly eroding the rock patiently.

The sand was exposed by the returning tide. White horses raced across the breakers, pleasing the surfers that bobbed and balanced eagerly in the shallows. The muted roar of the sea could just be heard even from the layby and the sea air was carried on the stiff inward breeze, declaring it presence and alerting all the senses of where they were. They could see the waves, taste and smell the salt in the air, hear the breakers and feel the sand in the wind. They were at the edge of an ocean, witnessing its effortless beauty.

David rolled the half open window right to the bottom and hung his arm out into the warm breeze.

"So what else do you have to tell me?" he asked.

Molly's head had dipped like she had been caught in some elaborate lie, which was not far from the truth, and had the unbearable weight of shame pushing her into the seat.

"I want you to know first, that everything between you and me is real" her voice broke as she uttered the words, she spat them out rapidly as if saying them quickly would make everything more believable, "Your father talked about you all the time and I fell in love with the idea of you before I even met you."

David said nothing.

"In reality, you were beyond what I imagined. I've been waiting to meet someone like you my whole life. You have all the best bits of your father and none of the bad.." her words were cut short.

"The bad? Is that what you are trying to tell me about? I had my mother tell me for years about how bad he was." There was disappointment woven into his voice. "I suppose you are going to tell me he was another kind of bad. I've made peace with my abandonment issues and I forgave him for not being in my life. Are you going to rip apart the image I have of my father? Destroy the brief relationship I had with him?"

He paused to collect his thoughts and drag them from the furthest corners of his mind. There was so much that needed to be said but maybe now was not the time to say it all. Perhaps letting Molly say her piece might change things, how he felt and how they would move forward. He had to say something of value.

"Look, I'm so blessed to have met you. I think you are incredible. You really have rocked my world. I may have lost my father, but I found you instead and so far I feel so much more of a connection to you than I ever did with him." His voice was softer now, "Say what you have to say. As long as it doesn't change anything between us then I'm sure it will be OK."

Molly's face said anything but 'it will be OK.' Her breathing was shallow and it seemed she might fall into the bottomless pit of a panic attack at any moment. David gripped her hand to let her know it would be alright. She looked up at him with those impossible eyes and feigned a smile. It would be the last for some time.

"Like I said, your father was being hunted by a professional, but he knew it was going to happen." A single tear rolled down her cheek, "He was prepared for it and he knew who had ordered it."

Molly started in earnest and told as much of the story as she knew from the beginning. John Hill had indeed been a brickie and general labourer for the first few years of his working life. He was a grafter, keen to show his skills and learn new ones as he gained more experience. The dream was to work for himself and be his own boss.

It was not the intention to walk away from his baby son forever, but he needed to get away from Pam, David's mother. She was like a leech, sucking the life out of the young man's dreams. He figured he would go away for a while, live a little, expand his horizons and be in a better position to be a good father. But it was not as simple as that, as it often never is.

John met up with a young Irish labourer, Phil Dobbs, and the two quickly became friends. They worked together, drank together and dreamed of making it big together. As a pair, they always seemed to be working for someone else. The money was not bad but not as good as it could be if they worked for themselves. They both had goals, John to be able provide for his son and Dobbs to send as much as he could back to his girlfriend in Northern Ireland.

After serving their time with a couple of building firms in the South West of England, Hill and Dobbs thought it was time that they tried to venture out on their own and put out the feelers to see if they could pick up a few odd jobs to fund a possible change in circumstances. As it happened, they did alright.

The jobs started to roll in and the pair set up their own firm; H & D Building and Property Maintenance. Life was on the up.

Although they had regular work, the jobs were building walls, laying paths and general home maintenance. They were waiting to land themselves that one big job that would have the massive return and maybe the recommendations for them to acquire other more lucrative work.

One Friday afternoon Hill and Dobbs had been building a wall for a garage owner who kept having his fences cut down and the stock of his second hand cars stolen. The money for the job was pretty decent and as long as they kept getting jobs like that they would be doing ok.

The garage owner had said that an associate of his was looking for 'some good men to do a job'. Maybe this was the next step in their success story.

The address they had been given was for a house on the outskirts of Bristol and the name of the man that was looking for 'some good men' was Duncan Bailey.

Back in those days Duncan Bailey was a young entrepreneur or that's what he told everyone. What his business was, nobody exactly knew. He traded in shotguns but the few gun sales he had was not enough to fund the lifestyle he seemed to have.

Bailey employed H & D to build him a bespoke garage and a new higher perimeter wall to his property. Hill was concerned by the spec of the garage. It had to accommodate at least two transit sized vans and have hidden compartments built into the walls, ceiling and floors. Bailey wanted them to work off plan and build it without there being any kind of blueprint or schematic to follow. Had there not been an upfront payment of the complete job, or Bailey using his many contacts to open a line of credit with builder's merchants, then the pair might have walked away. And in many times over the years since then they wish they had.

They were a couple of weeks into the job and seemed to have a queue of bigger and better jobs pencilled into their books for the coming months. There was the definite feel that all the hard work was starting to pay off and their dream would be realised. The future was looking up.

One evening, Bailey asked Hill if he knew any good drivers.

"HGV? Forklift? What kind of driver are you after?" John asked naively.

"Well more like a race car driver really" Bailey explained, "I have an interest in a bit of stock car racing and I need a good driver." It was a lie.

"Phil is a good driver. He does some track days and stock car driving." Hill motioned over to his friend and colleague who mixed cement at the other side of the construction site.

Bailey called over to the young Irishman and asked him if he would be interested in driving for him. With the promise of some good money, the answer was a resounding yes. Neither of the men knew Bailey's true intentions but it would soon become clear.

About a week later Bailey asked the pair if they would like to earn themselves 'a cool grand in cash' for one night of work, Dobbs as a driver and Hill to 'move some items'. The pair jumped at the chance to make some easy money and did not ask too many questions. That was ok though, Bailey filled them in fully on the job. He told them that a former business partner had stolen some of his stock and he was going to get it back using any means possible.

They left Bailey's house at midnight and Dobbs was told to drive into the city. It was just the three of them, Bailey sat in the back of the beaten up Volvo estate he had insisted they use. There was no conversation on the way. Bailey seemed edgy.

Once they arrived in the centre of the town, Bailey directed Dobbs to a dark back alley and got him to stop the car at the rear of a store.

The instructions were for Dobbs to keep the engine running and for Hill to follow Bailey into the store. But first, Bailey broke into the store. Hill thought he was in too deep to stop now and entered the store behind the man paying him to be there. Under flashlight, the store was clearly a gun shop. Bailey went from cabinet to cabinet and prised them open with a crowbar and broke off the security chains that ran through the trigger guards of all the displayed weapons. He filled sacks with the guns and handed them to Hill to load into the car. After several minutes and a few more trips, they were done and back in the car.

That was the first job and it was not to be the last. Store break-ins turned into house break-ins, house break-ins turned to petrol station raids. The crime started to escalate until there was a bigger crew pulling bigger jobs. Eventually, bank jobs, cash point machines, security vans, the works; the jobs got more and more sophisticated. So much so that one of the bigger criminal gangs started to take an interest.

Dougie Burnham was an old school leg breaker from London who had moved to Bristol to be a bigger fish in a smaller pond. He had a finger in every pie on the menu; robbery, prostitution, fraud and drugs. But he was not getting any younger and it was harder to keep up with all the smaller gangs that were taking ever increasing bites out of his business. As a shrewd yet ruthless operator, Burnham decided he would try to take some of the gangs under his wing and make them offers that they could not refuse.

Bailey was one such person that was approached. Not approached with an offer of a drink and a chat but dragged off the street and bundled into the back of a van by masked men. He would have been a fool to refuse or fight such an invitation. Pretty soon Bailey's crew were working Burnham's jobs. The cut was smaller but the jobs were much more lucrative so the take for each man was actually more than before.

Hill and Dobbs were still able to maintain their building firm but made far more money from the criminal activities they were involved in. Not to rely on the illicit gravy train, they ploughed much of the ill-gotten gains back into the firm to create the perfect façade. They had a work force, premises and equipment. Even if they were not able to take on as much business as they had first dreamed of, the overall appearance was a look of a successful, thriving construction company.

The years passed with a big job here and a few smaller ones there. Bailey had his gun shop and was deeply involved in that but trying to keep his hand in the criminal business, plus helping facilitate the needs of other gangs more so than his own. Dobbs was still a driver for hire and commanded a very good rate for his services. Hill on the other hand was keeping his head down and working hard at evading trouble with the law and hiding the money that he and Dobbs earned outside of the building business.

This thorough attitude did not go unnoticed by Burnham. Burnham liked Hill and Dobbs but was not fond of Bailey. He thought Bailey as spineless. However, he liked the work ethic that the building partners had and made them an offer they could not refuse, but this time the approach was made with a knock on the door and a cup of tea. There were no masked men anywhere in sight.

The discussion was done and the deal was in place. H & D Construction as it was now called was the main means to launder all the earnings for all of Burnham's criminal gangs. Of course, the Construction Company took a cut. By the time John Hill hit his fortieth birthday he was a millionaire, Phil Dobbs too.

Chapter Fifty Five

Jones had driven for quite some time, but now he needed to find a place to stop. The body in the boot was no longer unconscious and was kicking the panels, obviously trying to catch somebody's attention or escape.

Luckily, Jones had checked out the area the night before using satellite imagery from the internet and knew there was an abandoned airfield less than a mile along the road as this was the intended locality for interrogation.

He pulled off the road and through a gap in the hedge. The broken remains of the auxiliary roads were made of white concrete and had weeds growing in big clumps out of the many potholes in the surface. It was impossible not to hit the weeds and they could be heard brushing against the underside of the car. The activity in the boot had died down, as if the occupant knew that they would be stopping soon.

Jones manoeuvred the car into a small corrugated iron and concrete hanger at the edge of the now defunct runway. The floor was littered with chunks of rubble, rusted pieces of the corrugated skin of the building and weeds; the weeds grew everywhere.

With the boot opened from inside the car, Jones got out to see his captive struggling to escape without the use of his hands. The cable ties had held.

Jones pressed the muzzle of the Glock against Tom's temple and ripped off the tape from his mouth.

"Don't speak!" Jones said. He roughly dragged the bound man from the back of the car and stood him up.

"What do you…" Tom's question was cut short by a backhand to the face.

"What part of 'Don't speak' do you not understand?" Jones asked.

"The 'Don't' par.." another backhand. "Part." He finished.

A punch to the solar plexus dropped Tom to his knees. Jones rolled his eyes and lifted the man back to his feet.

"Anymore?" Jones asked.

"I can't sing or.." A punch to the jaw interrupted the quip, "Or Dance."

Another strike to the midsection dropped Tom back onto the floor. Jones left him in the dirt this time. As Tom coughed to try and get the air back in his lungs, Jones retrieved a rusted steel chair from the corner of the hanger and placed it near the fallen man.

In one swift action, Jones lifted Tom from the floor and dropped him on the seat. He then reached into the boot of the car and pulled out the long package.

"What's in here?" Jones asked.

"Can I speak now?" Tom said sarcastically.

"I'm gonna fucking shoot you if you don't answer my questions." Jones said brandishing the gun.

"Open it! We'll both get a surprise."

"Who sent it to you?" Jones pulled the knife out of his sock.

"You what?" Tom had genuine confusion spread across his face, "It's not for me."

Jones stepped closer and rested the muzzle of the Glock against Tom's knee.

"Then why is your name on it?" Jones asked the question in a hushed tone that barely contained his growing anger.

Tom leaned closer to his assailant's face.

"That's not my name." The statement was whispered but it screamed defiance.

Instead of a bullet through the knee cap, a whip of his gun hand had Jones expressing his contempt.

"Stop bullshitting me Hill," there was no restraint in his voice, "I saw you helping your dad's bitch out of the church. I checked out where you lived and the address matched where this package was delivered. And to top it off, I found you there."

"I'm not David Hill dickhead, you've fucked up big style." Tom laughed an ironic laugh.

"Who are you then? Elvis? Tom Jones, maybe? Are you gonna give me a quick verse of The Green Green Grass of Home or something?" Jones laughed his own, almost psychopathic, laugh but could not cover up the rage he felt.

"My name is Tom McDonald." He said, still maintaining a sense of defiance, "I have ID in my pocket."

Jones patted down Tom's jeans and then pulled a shabby leather wallet from the front pocket. He examined the driving license. If it was fake it was good, but somehow Jones believed the joker he had sitting in the chair.

"FUCK!" He said out loud.

"What next Cochise? I'm all bound up with nowhere to go." Tom could not help himself.

Jones paused to weigh up the situation. He had made the mistake. He had taken the wrong man and killed one of the neighbours too. The body count was growing on this job but then it was going to be a profitable one once it was finished. Would one more body matter? Maybe, maybe not, the next move would be crucial.

The decision was made. He placed the muzzle against Tom's forehead. His knuckle whitened with the pressure he applied against the trigger. At least the man in the chair was quiet for once.

Chapter Fifty Six

The information swirled in David's head. His father had been laundering money for an entire criminal network and his participation had made him a target.

They sat in silence for a moment until an off road vehicle parked right next to them. A small child pulled faces through the window of the huge four by four. The mother could be heard telling the child to behave while the father jumped out and started taking pictures of the vista that presented itself to all comers, those seeing it for the first were generally compelled to immortalise the view to digital memory.

"Shall we park elsewhere?" Molly said breaking silence.

"Sure. I know a place." David's voice seemed distant.

Molly had to negotiate the avid photographer father before driving down the hill towards the beach. David instructed her to turn left and take the road that ran parallel to the pebble bank that dominated the top of the beach.

The car crested the hump at the highest part of the road and the whole of the beach became visible. At low tide the beach stretched out to just short of three miles of flat sand. It was a perfect place to take a stroll and let the cool sea breeze lift all your troubles away. If you needed to disappear from the world for a few hours then this was the place to do it.

The car continued along at beach level for a short while and then started to climb up the narrow road as it hugged the contours of the coastline. Two small cars may pass each other easily enough but anything bigger would require a passing place, such was the width of the road.

The beach vanished from view as the hedges that divided the road from the cliffs were taller than the car. A car travelling in the opposite direction slowed down to let the Fiesta pass. It was almost claustrophobic as the two vehicles were just inches apart. Loose foliage from the hedge scraped against the door on the nearside. Once the vehicle had gone Molly accelerated up the brow of the hill until the road flattened out.

"Turn in here." David pointed to a small carpark on the right hand side of the road. There were no other vehicles so Molly parked up next to the left hand hedge where the car would be obscured from the road. She switched off the engine and turned to David.

"What next?" It was a valid question.

"I don't get you?" David asked.

"What do you want to know next? What do you want to do next?"

He pondered on that for a moment. What was to happen next? There was still the matter of the psychotic brothers that were following them. If they were following then who else could be out there looking for a piece of the action.

"What's on that laptop?"

"For want of a better phrase; your inheritance,"

"Explain?" He was none the wiser.

"Everything you'll ever need." The statement was ambiguous at best.

"I don't understand, what is on it?"

Molly reached back and lifted the case off the backseat and dumped it into his lap and opened up the front pocket. There was a driving licence, passport and several credit and debit cards. All the details were in the name of Steven Bowman but the face in the photo ID was David's.

"Who is Steven Bowman?"

"You are?" Her voice was deadpan.

That declaration silenced David once more but the quiet was very quickly interrupted as an old beaten up Transit van pulled in behind their parked car. They both knew who it belonged to. As if to compound the situation, David's phone started to ring. It was Tom's number that filled the screen. With eyes on the driver of the van, the phone was answered. A voice at other end of the line spoke. It was not Tom.

Chapter Fifty Seven

Molly started the ignition and tried to swiftly turn the car to escape but the van had been angled to block the entrance. Jimmy leapt from the cab and pointed the Browning directly at Molly. Words were not required, she took her hands of the wheel and held them up.

David had ignored the voice on the phone initially but now responded.

"Who is this?" David asked.

"Not important. I need to know if you have a laptop in your possession." The voice echoed.

"Look, we've got a big man with a gun pointing at us at the moment, so call back..." It may have sounded like he was joking but David could not have been more serious as his eyes tracked the firearm as Jimmy walked around to his side of the car.

"Is it a large bastard called Kinsella?" was the sardonic response "If it is, put him on."

David could not reply as the muzzle of the Jimmy's pistol tapped on the glass. The window rolled down and before Kinsella could say anything David handed him the phone.

"It's for you."

Confused, Jimmy took the phone and placed it against his ear.

"Hello?" he said in his gruff West Country twang.

"Ah, Jimmy. How is your brother? Not bleeding too much from all his bullet holes I hope?" The voice at the other end could be heard by all as Jimmy had accidentally hit speaker phone.

"YOU FUCKER! Where are you?" Jimmy screamed.

"Now, now Jimmy, calm down," a psychopathic laugh mingled with the words, "We can help each other out."

"How?" he shouted reply.

"I have a shotgun here which I believe you're after."

Jimmy paused. 'Time to shine' flashed through his mind.

"Go on." His gruff voiced mellowed slightly.

"The couple have a laptop in their possession and I want it."

"What's it worth?" Jimmy said feeling bolder, thinking he was holding a card the hitman wanted.

"To you nothing, but to my employer, quite a bit," The voice at the end of the phone said, "secure the couple the best you can and bring the laptop to me. Then you can have the shotgun as long as you don't try anything. Agreed?"

"Agreed."

The details of where, when and how were given and Jimmy hung up the phone. He levelled the old firearm at the couple ordering them out of the car and to bring the laptop with them.

David tried not to make any sudden movements. He did not want to take a bullet because he sneezed or something similar as the man pointing the gun at him appeared to be very twitchy.

Molly quaked where she stood.

"How did you find us?" It was as much as she could muster.

Jimmy did not answer her. He merely walked around the car, grabbed David by the scruff of the neck and dragged him to the rear of the car.

"Taped to the exhaust," Jimmy said in his deep smoker's voice, "rip it off and give it to me."

David did as he was told and dropped to his knees. There was something heavily wrapped in duct tape and attached to the end of the tail pipe. It was a mobile phone. Clearly, this lump of a man was smarter than he looked. He had used a mobile phone location App to find them.

David handed him the phone and then followed Jimmy over to the van. There were no words spoken, just gestures with the muzzle of the gun. Molly nervously edged toward the vehicle too.

Jimmy opened the side door and ushered them both in. His obviously injured brother was propped up in the corner trembling. Billy looked pale and tired, a fine sweat covering his face.

"Turn away from me and put your hands behind you backs." The command was given with a prod of the gun into David's ribs.

They did as they were told. There was another player in the game now and who knew which way this was going to go. David could see Molly was petrified. There were no words he could say to ease her fear.

Their wrists were bound with duct tape, he presumed the same tape that attached the phone to the exhaust, and then a piece was placed across their mouths. Molly snuggled in as close as she could to David. Just to feel a modicum of the protection she so desperately needed.

Jimmy handed the pistol to his brother and sat him opposite the couple in the payload bay.

"If either moves, shoot them! But only in the leg or the arm, we might need them alive." Jimmy delivered the instructions the same way as a parent would to a small child. "It won't be long now. Soon we'll be rich and I can get you fixed up. I'll even get you a private nurse, a pretty one too."

Billy just nodded his head. It was obviously an effort for him to hold the gun. His hand trembled so much that he rested the weapon against his good knee to aim it toward them.

The older brother jumped out the side door and slammed it shut. The noise echoed like the sealing of a tomb. Maybe that is what the van was to become, a tomb, maybe for one, maybe for them all. When the van next stopped the game would change, that was for sure. But in whose favour would remain to be seen.

Chapter Fifty Eight

The damp air of the hanger was acrid. Tom thought that maybe he should slow his breathing to stop taking in the foul air but his heart was beating too fast, he needed the oxygen. He was not sure why the man with the gun had thought better of killing him. After all he had taken Tom by accident. Surely one less witness was a good thing.

Tom watched as the hitman examined the shotgun. There was something in the barrels that the man wanted. The man looked around on the floor of the hanger. He spotted something and walked over to it. Tom watched as the man picked up a long piece of tough wire and fed it into one of the barrels of the weapon. Something dropped to the floor. The man repeated the action on the other barrel until another item dropped out.

The man was clearly very cautious. He did not immediately pick up the items. He dropped the wire and pulled out a knife. There was a lot of prodding with the tip of a knife before they were picked up.

Although Tom could not really see what fell out of the shotgun but soon it was pretty clear what they were. The man had retrieved a laptop from the back seat of the BMW and placed it on the boot. Once the screen had flickered on, the man slipped one of the items into a USB port, obviously a pair of data sticks had been secreted into the barrels.

"Son of a bitch!" Jones exclaimed.

"Celebrity sex tape?" Some of Tom's bravado was returning.

"I can still shoot you, you know?" Jones' eyes did not leave the screen as he answered.

"I know, but I guess you're a smart guy and keeping me alive is to your advantage."

"I am a smart guy."

"I know. You were probably top of the class in Hitman School." Tom could not help himself sometimes.

"I was top of the class in marksman school. I could pop a bullet through one of your lungs from here, which would stop you from talking but not necessarily kill you. So if you don't mind shutting the fuck up while I copy these files then that would be great." Jones returned the banter but with a far more chilling outcome.

"Ok, I will but do you all drive big black German cars like they do in the movies, or is there a choice, like a mercenary car pool or something?"

The Glock was drawn and pointed directly at Tom's head.

"Say another word, I dare you."

There was nothing but silence for the next ten minutes. Tom observed the gunman's expression change as he read more revelations from the data sticks. The facial giveaways were somewhere between surprise and admiration. There was an appreciation for somebody's handiwork but who and why would remain mystery for now.

Tom had other things on his mind. He had discovered a rough edge on the seat of the rusty chair he was bound to. As carefully as he could, he dragged the cable ties back and forth against it. It took time as the movements could only be an inch at a time but eventually he made some progress and the tie snapped. What he would do next would have to wait. A vehicle could be heard approaching.

"Did you order pizza? I'm starving!" Tom offered.

"No, but I ordered you some company." Jones replied as he took position near to the hangar door.

Chapter Fifty Nine

Outside the hangar entrance was as far as the van would go. The side door whizzed open. Jimmy had climbed over the seat into the payload bay to retrieve the gun. His brother looked visibly worse than twenty minutes ago when he handed him the firearm. It would be the end of Billy if he did not receive any medical attention soon.

Jimmy ushered David and Molly out of the van whilst picking up the laptop bag. He stood behind them as he made them walk into the hangar still bound and gagged. If there was an ambush he was going to use them as a shield.

There was no ambush but as Jimmy walked in through the wide opening he could see the black BMW and Tom apparently tied to a chair. This was enough of a distraction as a piece of cold steel was pushed against the side of his head.

"Hello Jimmy," Jones had the drop on him. The pressure of the Glock was not welcoming and neither was the greeting, "Is that for me?" taking the laptop from Jimmy's hand.

"Where's the shotgun?" Jimmy asked.

"Hand me your firearm first."

Jimmy did as he was told. He did not have his brother to take another bullet for him.

"Wow! A Browning high power," there was a mix of mild admiration and intense sarcasm in the comment "they don't make them like this anymore. A bit like you and your brother, how is Billy by the way?"

"You've got what you want. Let me have what I want and I'll be on my way." Jimmy had to curtail his rage.

"It's in the boot of my car. You can help yourself."

Jimmy walked passed David and Molly toward the rear of the vehicle. It was not locked. He popped the catch and could see his prize lying on the plastic sheeting that lined the boot.

"Happy?" Jones asked.

"I think so," Jimmy said. He reached in and lifted the weapon. It was heavier than it looked.

"Do you know what it is?"

Jimmy looked puzzled but the question was valid. All the chaos and killings of the last week or so had surrounded the hunk of steel and wood in his hands but he still did not know its significance.

"It's a valuable shotgun." He answered naively.

"It's worth about two grand, tops." Jones' mocking smile did not give away the truth so he filled the older, not necessarily wiser, brother in to its true value. "What it contained was worth far more."

The two data sticks were identical copies of financial transactions, funds that had been skimmed off the top of

Burnham's money laundering scheme. Even though John Hill's business was the main funnel for all moneys, some transactions had used other connected business ventures, one of them being The Gunroom and several other fictitious companies which were all listed as being owned, part owned or co-owned by Duncan Bailey, James Kinsella, Jimmy Kinsella, William Kinsella, Billy Kinsella and William Fegan. All the names and aliases used by Bailey and the Kinsellas in some of their known criminal activity. The data sticks contained detailed records of all the connected businesses, whether they were Hill's or Bailey's.

The transactions stretched back almost twenty years and accounted for upwards of ninety million pounds of illegal money but everything that had passed through John Hill's Construction Company was exact and precise. Every tool, brick or nail was properly accounted for. The ins and outs of the business were extremely detailed.

The dealings through all of the Bailey/Kinsella businesses were far more random. There were too many unexplained costs and expense variances. Some were subtle in as much as 'coffee, milk and sugar = £25' to a refit at The Gunroom which costs in excess of £100,000 and another which cost £125,000. Anybody who had been in the store could see that there had been no major works to improve the site since the doors had opened other than a lick of paint and some new lighting.

The information had Bailey skimming far more than he was entitled to over a very long period of time. If this data was to get back to Burnham then it would spell the end of Bailey and the Kinsellas. It would also show the motive to have John Hill killed as he could have discovered and verified the activity. With Hill dead the deception could continue and possibly the previous deceit may have never been discovered. Also new leads could be created to implicate Hill in the con.

"So there we have it. Your boss was ripping everyone off and was too stupid to cover his tracks well enough, also implicating you and your brother in many of the deals." Jones maintained the same sneering smile as he delivered the bombshell.

Jimmy's mouth dropped open as he stared down at the weapon in his hands. Its purpose had been far more damaging than its original design. He had been chasing the method of his downfall. There was never going to be a 'Time to Shine,' that had already been decided. Jimmy could have taken his brother and ran but instead they were wrongly searching for the one thing that would seal their fate.

"What next?" Jimmy asked on a low voice, his spirit broken.

"Well I've emailed the files to my employer and I'm waiting on the answer on that..." the sentence was interrupted by a vibration from Jones' pocket. He carefully took his phone out, never lowering his gun or taking his eyes off Jimmy the whole time. He raised the phone so he could read the text without moving his head. The smile on his face widened once more, "Unlucky Jimmy!"

Two rounds from the Glock hit Jimmy centre mass and instantly he was on the ground. His groans were like a whimper of a stricken animal that knows its time is up.

Jones walked over to the fallen man.

"All of your life, people have decided your fate and now I'm no different."

Jimmy lifted his eyes to meet his aggressor but it was all the fight he had left. A final round through the forehead ended Jimmy Kinsella's life.

Chapter Sixty

As the sound of the final gunshot dissipated into the old framework of the disused hangar, the full horror of their predicament sank deep into their collective consciousness. David tried to speak but the tape was still firmly sealing his lips. He watched as Jones picked up the fallen Browning pistol.

Jones then walked over to David and Molly and ripped the tape from their mouths. He then turned them around and cut the tape on their wrists.

"How much did you know about this scam?" Jones asked as if he was asking someone for the time. Not like a man who had just ended someone's life. Death must be a daily occurrence in this man's existence.

"Nothing." was David's brief answer.

"Excuse me a moment." Jones said walking out to the van. They saw him peer into the darkness of the side payload door. He raised the Glock and fired a single round. They presumed he was finishing Billy off. It was a mercy killing as the younger brother was near death as it was.

"Sorry about that," he said as he returned to the petrified group, "one loose end tied off and now to finish everything else off."

"Why are you doing this?" David asked.

"Because I'm being paid to"

"What if we could pay more?" Molly piped up.

"Firstly, you couldn't afford me. Secondly, I've been paid to do one job and if I fail that job then I'll end up like him," he gestured toward Jimmy Kinsella's corpse. He delivered the words is if it was no big deal.

"You haven't checked the laptop yet. Are you going to?" David was trying to buy them some time.

"I will but it won't change the plan but if you're curious I'll do it now." Jones casually picked up the laptop bag and walked toward the rear of the BWM. He closed the boot and rested the bag on top.

As he was about to unzip the bag Tom lunged from the seat and launched himself at the hitman. Tom caught him in the centre of the back with a shoulder. Jones staggered against the car but did not fall.

David joined in the attack and jumped onto the man's back.

It seemed not to matter, Jones would not go down. He swiped out with his gun hand and caught Tom on the side of the face. Tom clattered back onto the chair he been restrained to.

Jones then reached up over his head, grabbed hold of David's neck and pulled him to the ground. He pointed the Glock directly at David's head but was suddenly hit from the side. The gun went off. David felt the shockwave pass his face by mere millimetres, the round impacted into the brittle concrete floor and threw up the fragments like shrapnel. Tom had swung the rusty chair into the hitman and it broke apart against the rigid physique of this seemingly unstoppable man.

David got to his feet and picked up the shotgun that had been lying with the body of Jimmy Kinsella. It was deactivated but made a good clubbing weapon. David gripped the barrel and swung the butt end into the stomach of their would-be killer. Jones dropped to the dirt for the first time, winded by the blow.

Seeing they had the advantage, Tom kicked Jones in the face and stamped his heel into the gun hand that was desperately trying to find a target. Jones lost grip and the gun slipped from his hand. David kicked the weapon away as far as he could and struck down on the fallen man with the shotgun once more.

With Jones face down, Tom leapt onto his back and hooked punches into both sides of the man's head.

"Get the girl and fuck off!" Tom shouted.

"No way!" David continued to beat down on the prone, motionless body.

"Go! Now!" Tom screamed this time.

"You don't need to be a hero" David shouted back as his attack paused.

"I'm not," The words were spoken, "take her and go."

David ceased his attack, dropped the shotgun and gripped Molly by the arm. She had been frozen with fear but now was spurred into moving.

"We need the laptop!" She said reaching for the forgotten item.

"LEAVE IT!" David shouted.

"WE NEED IT!" She shouted back at him.

David hooked the shoulder strap and took Molly's hand leading her quickly towards the door.

"LEAVE HIM TOM!" David urged his friend to follow them.

Tom paused, ceasing the attack for a moment.

"You go. I'll keep him busy." Tom said breathlessly.

"You're an asshole!" David said as he pulled Molly through the hangar door toward the van.

"I'm your asshole brethren." Tom hollered over his shoulder as he continued to punch the man beneath him.

The sunlight was blinding as they ran out of the dim hangar. David rushed to the van and opened the driver's side door. No keys. For a moment he thought to return to search the dead body but thought better of it. They had a head start and now was not the time to squander it.

"Come on," he said to Molly, "let's see how we fair on foot."

They headed as fast as they could along the potholed path toward the main road.

Tom started to tire. His fists were beginning to hurt. The punches had slowed considerably.

Jones seized his chance and pushed himself up with his powerful arms. Tom was bucked off, falling back onto the debris covered hangar floor.

Rapidly leaping to his feet, Jones reached down and grabbed Tom by the neck of his T-shirt, lifting the smaller man from the floor and then punched him squarely on the chin. Stunned, Tom fell back to the ground and did not move.

Jones quickly scanned for the Glock. He ran to the weapon, swiftly picked it up and sprinted out of the hangar after the absconding couple. He could see them heading toward a small sentry box near the opening to the road. A shot on the run would be no good. There was only one chance to get this right.

He skidded to a halt and cupped his left hand under the butt of the gun for stability. Jones squeezed the trigger. One shot. He rarely missed. This time was no different.

The adrenaline pumped through their veins as the road grew closer. It seemed to take forever, like in slow motion. The small brick sentry box that marked the opening to the road was only a ten yards or so away when David heard something behind him. He chose not to look back.

As they finally pulled level with the sentry box and started to turn the corner there was a loud crack; a gunshot maybe.

David felt something like sledgehammer hit him in the ribs. He was lifted off his feet and fell onto the dirt. He had been shot.

Chapter Sixty One

Tom got to his feet. The ache that throbbed through his jaw was unlike anything he had ever felt before. He doubted whether had ever been hit so hard.

Outside he could hear the fast paced padding of sprinting on concrete. It just occurred to him that he was alone in the hangar. The blow must have stunned him enough for the hitman to leave to give chase to his friends without Tom knowing anything about it.

Discarded on the boot lid was the old Browning pistol that Jimmy had been woefully unprepared to use. Tom picked it up.

As he started to run toward the exit he heard the crack of a gunshot outside. The sound was very different than the deafening echo of the previous shots that ended the Kinsellas. It was a chilling sound regardless of the environment. Somewhere there was piece of metal flying faster than the speed of sound, its only purpose to maim or kill.

Tom could see the hitman standing twenty or so yards ahead of him aiming the gun. The bend in the path stopped Tom from seeing what was happening at the edge of the site but he figured it would not be pleasant. He raised the Browning, took aim and fired.

He missed.

The round must have passed close to Jones' head. The hitman ducked, and turned toward the sound of the gunshot.

Tom adjusted his aim and fired again. Closer, but he missed again. He was suddenly aware that he was standing in the open and lunged for cover behind the Transit van.

Another gunshot, but this time the sound did not come alone. A pain akin to a searing hot blade hit Tom in the right shoulder. He dropped the gun.

The van was the only thing between Tom and another bullet. His right arm was now useless. He picked up the gun in his left hand. With two poor attempts with his dominant hand, he did not fancy his chances with his left. He tried to scramble to his feet and seek shelter back in the hangar but as he cleared the gap between the van and the entrance another bullet caught him in the hip.

He fell hard onto the cold damp floor. The sensation was like been hit by a car. Blood flowed from a large wound at the top of his leg. Unable to stand, he rolled on to his back and fought through the pain to aim the pistol toward the door. He rested the pistol against his knee and prayed for a hit if he was able to get another shot off.

The dull black metal of the Glock appeared around the edge of the wide doorway, closely followed by Jones' face. The delay was all the time Tom needed to make good his aim.

A single shot was loosed from the old WW2 pistol. The round clipped the edge of the hangar door splintering the brittle concrete and taking some of the power out of the bullet, but it still hit its target.

The ricochet hit Jones in the left side of his chest. He flinched but retaliated with two rounds. Both found their target.

Tom groaned as the bullets ripped through his torso. The gun fell from his hand. His resolve had come to an end.

Jones stepped into the hangar. The Glock was levelled at Tom as he struggled to breathe, blood trickled from the corner of his mouth.

"You hit me!" Jones said with the same sneering smile on his face, "In the chest as well."

"I was…aiming for…your fucking head!" Tom battled to breathe.

"Your friend was right, you are an asshole."

"Yeah…but…I'm not your asshole…" He could resist death no longer. Tom's last breath was spent on a quip for his killer. Had he died in vain or had his efforts bought his friends the time to get away? Either way he perished doing his best.

Chapter Sixty Two

David rolled in the dirt and out of the line of fire. He patted down the side of ribs where he felt the bullet impact. There was no blood, only an intense pain. He looked at Molly's horrified face as she stood over him, desperately trying to pull him to his feet, she pointed to the laptop bag. There was smoke escaping from a bullet hole in the bag.

Another gunshot rung out, the pitch was different than the first. Again another but it was quickly followed by a gunshot that sounded like the first one fired at them. There was no time to see what was happening back at the hangar. They had to run, now, while they could.

The single track lane was flanked by tall, overgrown hedgerows. If they were pursued by car there would be no escape for them. Several more shots rang out but they sounded muffled, as if fired inside. There was no time to turn back. No decision to return and help. David knew that they were running for their lives and no amount of bargaining could help them now.

After a hundred yards or so of impassable dense foliage on either side of the road, they came to a gate. David paused to catch his breath. The slug that had been stopped by the laptop had still made its presence felt. Each breath hurt like hell so maybe there was a broken rib or two that would have to be dealt with later.

"There's a house at the far end of the field." Molly said.

Sure enough there was a small whitewash cottage with smoke billowing out of an oversized chimney in the opposite corner of the field. There might be someone who could help them or maybe just a place to hide for a while.

"Ok, let's go?" David said climbing over the steel gate. "We need to get off the road."

There was no argument from Molly as she duly followed. The pair kept low and tight to one of the hedges, using the natural cover it provided. The hope was that they would not be seen by a vehicle from the road or the sharp eyes of a killer with a pistol in his hand.

Their decision to get off the road could not have been more timely, as the roar of a high power vehicle wheel spinning somewhere behind them, spurring them on to run harder to get to the cottage. Where the car, if it was THE car, was going could not be determined but soon the sound of the engine was running parallel to the hedgerow. In seconds it was off into the distance.

As they approached the dwelling, they could see the back door was open and a small blonde woman was sat on a deckchair taking in the sun's rays, wearing headphones and oblivious to the happenings so near to her house.

"Hello," David called to the woman, "could we use your telephone?" He tried not to appear nervous for his own live but feared he was failing miserably.

"Oh, hello." The women pulled the headphone buds from her ears and replied as if it was commonplace to have random strangers trudging across the field, "Sorry I didn't hear what you wanted."

"A phone, can we use it?" David repeated.

"I'm sorry I don't have a landline. Have you not got a mobile? Some of them work out here."

David looked at his phone and sure enough his signal had creeped up to two bars. While standing in a field at the edge of an unfamiliar house he decided to make a call.

"Who are you calling?" Molly asked.

"The Police."

"And tell them what? We have to run or hide David. The police can't help us here."

"There's at least two dead bodies up the road, and a killer on the loose. And then there's Tom. What's happened to him?" David felt such guilt for leaving his friend behind even if it was what he was instructed to do. The loyal friendship that had bonded them had now separated them, with the extent of his friend's sacrifice yet to be discovered, but life would never be the same again whatever the outcome. "I have to call or do something."

"David," She placed her hand on his, "Trust me, don't call them." Her voice was calm for the first time in about an hour.

He responded to her by putting his phone back in his pocket.

"Would you two like a lift into to town," The blond lady had removed herself from the chair and walked over to them, unaware of the exchange between the couple. "I'm just having a cup of tea. Would you like one?"

David looked at Molly and then across the field from where they had come from.

"Do you want a drink?" He asked Molly.

"We need to lie low for a bit and then get back to my car." She answered. There was something she was not telling him. David could sense it.

"We'd love a cuppa, thanks!" David said turning to the woman, who stood with her hands on her hips waiting patiently for their answer.

The woman directed them to the gate that led into the garden and then made her introduction. Within the first sentence of conversation she told them her life story, name; Jane, although she preferred Janey, kids; two, marital status; happily divorced. So friendly but then so was most of this part of the country. She continued to chat without a pause whilst making the drinks.

David and Molly sat in the snug on a very new two seater sofa trying to remain calm. Although the house looked like a rustic cottage from the outside it was more like a very modern show house on the inside. Newly polished wooden floors with expensive looking rugs dotted between the new furniture. Jane did explain as part of her chat that she had recently renovated the broken down old cottage and turned it into a regular country haven for her and her many visitors.

"How far is it to Newgale from here?" David asked the woman once she had finished preparing the drinks and came to join them.

"It's a couple of miles. I'll take you there. I don't mind, I've got nothing better to do." She laughed as if she her conversation was entertaining her guests.

They talked for a little while, small talk really, a few anecdotes about living in middle of nowhere from Jane, but little more than a few comments from David.

Molly just smiled and nodded. She said nothing. Her mind was elsewhere, playing with her phone whilst trying to appear interested in the constant conversation.

There was a knock at the front door. David and Molly looked at each other.

"Who could that be? I'm not expecting anyone," Jane got up and headed for the door.

Molly got to her feet and pulled David to his.

"We need to go." Her eyes were filled with fear again, the same fear that David had witnessed earlier.

They heard the door open and then Jane speak to whoever was calling. There was no acknowledgement to her greeting.

Suddenly David's hand dropped to his pocket. His phone was vibrating. It always vibrated just before it rang.

He tried to get the phone out of his pocket to see who was calling. As he pulled it free,'TOM' appeared across the screen. There was a nanosecond of relief that maybe his friend had made it out ok. But all thoughts of a positive outcome were quickly banished from his mind.

A gunshot rang out followed by a crash from the hallway.

Frozen to the spot by fear, David craned his neck slightly to look into the hall. Jane lay on the floor, a bullet hole through her forehead, her eyes still wide open.

Jones stood in the doorway, pistol in one hand, a mobile phone in the other; Tom's phone. His face was marked and bruised from the earlier beating, there was also a patch of blood on the right side of his chest but he still smiled the same psychopathic smile.

"Looks like I've caught you." There was relish in Jones' words.

He was right. They were well and truly caught.

Chapter Sixty Three

"Why don't you have a bullet hole in you?" Jones asked, his right eye was puffy and red from the beating, "I don't miss often and I'm sure I hit you."

David remained silent. This man had already tried to kill him and a careless quip could see him succeed at this short range.

"Cat got your tongue?" Jones turned and pointed the pistol at Molly, "What's the answer to this? Can you tell me?"

"You," her voice broke under the pressure of having a professional killer standing before her with his weapon of choice aimed directly at her head, "You h-hit the laptop."

"Wow! That was a bit of luck." There was no humour about the situation yet Jones had a sardonic smile for everything. He switched his attention back to David "You better open it up and check the damage. I need to know what's on it. I won't be happy if it doesn't work."

David reached down and unzipped the bag. He lifted out the shattered device. The bullet had entered the top side of the laptop puncturing the screen and continued through into the battery which was enough to stop the round from penetrating any further.

"If I had been using a round with a copper jacket, that would have gone all the way through and that lady in the hallway would still be alive because I would have got you back at the airfield." Jones laughed but not in a good way, much like a school bully preying on a weaker child and snickering sadistically.

The next instruction was to empty the full contents of the bag.

David carefully laid out everything on the nice new rug that the owner of the house would no longer be able to benefit from. Aside from the broken laptop there were two memory sticks, the same type that had been found in the shotgun, there was a thousand pounds in cash and two sets of identity; a passport, a driver's licence, birth certificate and bank card each in the names of Stephen Bowman and Rebecca Stowford. The photographs were of David and Molly.

"That's an expensive ID package." The hitman's expression changed from to sadistic to almost kudos, "You guys are well funded. What do you have to say about that?" The question was directed at David.

"I honestly don't know anything about those." It was the truth.

"Well, what about you," the Glock was again pointed in Molly's direction, "what have you got to say about all this? Do you know what is on those sticks? Do you know who funded those IDs?"

"I do," she started, "The sticks have all the financial records both fraudulent and genuine for H & D Construction, money transfers, hidden accounts, payment details, both for legal and illegal transactions, the whole inner workings of the business is a façade to conceal the scale of the criminal activity."

David stared at her in disbelief. She talked with confidence about the subject.

"Wow! You seem to know a lot about it." Jones said.

"I should do. I did all the accounts and handled all the paperwork. The files were created by me." Her fear seemed to have vanished, "I know everything there is to know about the entire crime network of the Burnham gang. I even know about you." Her statement was aimed at Jones.

"You don't know anything about me." A veil of rage fell across Jones' face, "You must have some balls trying to pull this shit."

"You're on the payroll, the same as the rest of the gang. We pay your handler and he pays you."

"My handler might be a woman!" Jones said defiantly.

"I know your handler personally. It's a man. You get a phone call with a target, a job and a price." Molly's confidence was bordering on arrogance.

"What's his name?" His face was boiling over. Normally he would have pulled the trigger by now but he knew that he had to find out more. An error here could spell the end of his career, and in his line of work. Notification for sacking would come in the form of a 9mm round through the back of the head.

"Steve Allen," she paused to see if there was a glimmer of recognition sparkle in the hitman's eyes. There was. "Or you may know him as Ducty?"

"The drug dealer?" the rage faded to incredulity. "What bullshit are you trying to feed me?"

"That's what you are meant to believe. He's supposed to look like a low-rent, sportswear covered drug dealer." The balance of power seemed to have shifted. Molly commanded the room. The hitman did not know what to think and whether there was any truth in what she said. "It's the perfect cover. If there is a contract completed by a professional in the city then they aren't going to look at someone peddling bags of weed on the rundown estates now are they?"

There was logic to her words. Ducty seemed to drift through life unscathed from other criminal activity, ever present but never arrested. There must have been some form of protection that his position afforded him.

"Then why was I hired to kill his father?" Jones gestured toward the stunned David. It was the first time it was confirmed. His father had died at the hands of the killer before them.

"Jay wanted out of the business. Meeting his son for the first time in decades made him realise that he had missed out on so much." Molly returned the gaze that she was now receiving silently from David. "He was done with doing the bidding of Dougie Burnham. He was done with having the likes of Duncan Bailey and the Kinsellas trying to muscle their way to the top of the pack, thinking they had more clout than they did. Bailey thought Jay owed him for putting him in the position of importance that he was. Jay thought it was a curse and wanted out long ago, but you don't just leave the Burnham Gang."

"So he wanted out of the business and killing himself was the only way to do that was it?" Jones was utterly confused now.

"In order to protect David it was a sacrifice worth making."

"Fucking stupid if you ask me," the gun had been lowered and the conversation had turned into a debate, "So I've killed his dad, half the organisation and a few innocents, including this poor bitch on the floor and your friend back at the hangar, just because John Hill wanted to quit."

There was no immediate reply. The news of Tom's murder had to sink in first. So much had been lost. Life is a fragile article. All the elements of these last couple of weeks had broken every piece of David's life. The existence he had come to expect was gone. It was like a shattered mirror. No matter how hard you looked at the reflection, all that you recognise could no longer be seen amongst the miniscule shards that remained. Going forward, those shards would have to be picked out of David's soul until none remained, then and only then, would some form of life return. And even then would it be one worth living?

"You joined the dots and killed everyone you came into contact with. This carnage is on you." It was the first thing David had said in what seemed like forever. "I hope it was worth the price."

"My conscious is clear and when I off you pair I will feel nothing." Jones said coldly. He raised the gun once more and pointed it centre mass toward David.

"I'm sure you won't," Molly interrupted, "but it would be foolish to kill us."

"Oh, and why is that?"

"You don't know the full extent of what is on these data sticks," she looked down at the neatly arranged items on the rug before them, "They're very valuable if you know how to use the information on them."

"Don't worry they'll be coming with me anyway." Jones said glibly.

"But you need us to access the accounts as we have all the correct ID requirements to get to it." Molly's voice had the nerves creeping back in.

"My ID is probably made by the same people that made yours. I can get all the fake papers I need to access the accounts." The sneering sadistic arrogance had returned along with the balance of power

"There's a lot of money in the various accounts, you'll need help."

"How much money?"

"Approximately five million pounds worth in various currencies," Molly said, "It will take some organisation to get it all quickly."

"Hmmm, it would make it easier for me in the long run but I'd have to babysit the pair of you until the funds were released." Jones raised the gun so that Molly had no choice but to stare down the barrel. "And that's something I'm not prepared to do."

"Oh well, you can't blame me for trying." Molly's words had a ring of sarcasm about them.

"Indeed, and you stupidly told me how much everything is worth." Jones stated.

"Oh that was to serve a purpose." She said defiantly.

"Eh, what purpose?" Jones asked.

"To kill time and distract you."

"What?" It was the last word he ever said.

A 9mm round passed straight through his skull from back to front, the bullet exited above his left eye, taking most of the upper part of his face with it. The killer's lifeless body fell forward and his prized Glock finally dropped from his dead hand.

Everything seemed to happen in slow motion. The sound of the gunshot, the body falling to the floor, and the recognition of the figure brandishing a gun in the still open doorway, it was like a dream. Could it be true?

"Come on kids. Let's get out of here before the police arrive." John 'Jay' Hill stood as large as life.

David just looked in awe. His feet did not or could not respond to the instruction. He looked at Molly in a daze. She merely grabbed his hand and pulled him toward the door. It was clear that this was no surprise to her.

As they passed John, David uttered one word.

"How?"

"There's no time to explain but I wasn't going to take my own life to escape the gang." He pushed his son through the open door.

Outside was a large old camper van. Phil Dobbs was at the wheel. Lorna sat next to him with a look of angst for the safety of her own daughter spread across her face.

David, Molly and Jay climbed in through the cabin door and into the comfort of the camper's living area.

Once the camper started moving it did not stop until the fuel was low. By then they had crossed all of Wales and most of the North of England. After refuelling the camper and themselves, all five crossed the border into Scotland together. New identities; New Lives, although tainted with all that had gone before. Would they ever find peace? Who knew? But they would at least try.

Chapter Sixty Four

Three Years Later.

The faltering steps and awkward gait, the feet swung widely, searching for the ground. A new sensation underfoot; the cold damp sand causing a curiosity about this strange place; a new experience committed to memory.

The line of footprints barely marking the surface but showed where someone had been and which way they were heading, walking into the unknown on this inexplicable terrain; a child's first steps on a beach.

Stephen and Rebecca Bowman walked hand in hand behind their son, Thomas McDonald Bowman. The infant's first birthday treat was a trip to his father's favourite place, Newgale beach. The endless sand stretched before them like the forthcoming years of their lives, afforded to them by the child's namesake. Fake names, but real lives built on real emotion.

This was the first return to Wales since that critical day. The day that everything changed; lives, names, identities, all altered in an instant.

In the days that followed those events, the details were fed slowly in small chunks like when feeding a child. The plan was not intricate but relied on a lot of luck and assumption.

Mouthful one was the plan to implicate Bailey and the Kinsellas. The hard part was to fake the records and create a false money trail directly to The Gunroom. The bogus break in caused interest, lies were told and rumours started. The curiosity in the items built as the second layer of deceit was laid over the break in. The Kinsellas were sacked from the site whilst digging for clues to the break in. Bailey knew he had been implicated in the robbery and that the items were part of the proof and he had asked the Kinsellas to see what they could find. One lie lead to another and Bailey was at the head of the queue as the one who ordered the hit on Hill. It was a lie. Hill had ordered his own death, using Ducty to his own advantage, plus a healthy payoff to keep it all undercover.

The biggest morsel to swallow was how John Hill had managed to fake his own death.

The faking was easier than first thought. When one of his workmen broke down and cried about being diagnosed with terminal cancer, Hill hatched a plan. The man was Paul Barnard and he was devastated about having to leave his beloved wife and three daughters to fend for themselves.

Both Hill and Barnard were in their fifties, roughly the same build and although not alike in many ways, they were similar enough to be mistaken for one another. Hill promised to look after Barnard's wife and kids if Barnard took the fall, so to speak, for him. A sweetener of one hundred thousand pounds in cash was given in good faith and the deal was done.

Barnard was well motivated as he knew the type of people that inhabited the criminal underworld and that if Hill came to any harm then Mrs Barnard would get nothing. Barnard went to the site and took the fall. Fake ID identified the body as John Hill and Phil Dobbs went to the mortuary to confirm that fact, even though Dobbs was not privy to the set up, he assumed that would be the correct thing to do and figure out the truth later. The plan was in motion.

Unfortunately, there were too many variables to maintain. There was one crucial mistake made by Dobbs which changed the whole outcome of the plan. He should have never sent the shotgun to David's address, only the laptop. In his panic he sent both items. Had the shotgun been found at the lock up then the search would have ended there and Jones would have ceased. Control over Jones was lost at that point. In an uncontrollable situation there will always be collateral damage. Jane, the lady from the cottage, Pete Flynn, Amble Goodrich, Rachel and Tom were all that; collateral damage.

David, or Stephen as had he was just getting used to, often thought about all that had happened to give him the life he now lived with the woman he loved. Was it worth it? Only time would tell but the life he was now living was the one bestowed upon him. It did not matter that he knew nothing of the plot. David had to maintain to the façade to preserve his new family. The fake death had created the fake life, funded by an illicit inheritance, the product of so many casualties. No one could ever escape unharmed from the carnage, not even the most innocent of participants would be free to live the life they want. But that was the risk of plan, John Hill's plan.

Hill only wanted to protect those closest and loyal to him. Sacrifices had to be made in order to make that happen. He would have to live with the result as did everyone else. Even after his eventual death, either from natural causes or otherwise, those left behind would have to accept the life he had bestowed upon them. This was his legacy.

The man leaned over the roof of the car. His binoculars picked up the small family group walking on the sand. It was definitely who he had been tasked to find. They had taken the risk of coming back out of hiding and he had found them.

The man did not care. It mattered not why these people were on the run, or why they had reappeared once more. All that mattered was the task.

After all, he was a gun for hire. He had received the call. The instructions came from an unknown source at the end of the phone. He was given a target, a job and a price. And he would not fail.

The End.

Feed an Author, Write a Review

Thank you for reading this book. If you have enjoyed this story then please recommend it to a friend and also look into the other titles by this author. If you would like to thank the author for their efforts in creating a story that has entertained you, then please return to the site from which you purchased this book and leave a review. Also, the author would be immensely grateful if you, the reader, would place a similar recommendation on sites such as Goodreads.com or maybe even place a link to the purchase page on your personal social media pages or any relevant group you follow.

Thank you once again.

My Gratitude

I would like to say thank you to all those that have supported me through the creation of this book. Thank you to all the readers of FROM WITHIN who have given me the strength and encouragement (and reviews) to continue on my writing journey and helped me through the tough times while writing THE LEGACY. Special thanks go to David Walker and Lauren Greenway for their input and reading THE LEGACY in its raw form.

For more information on forthcoming titles from the author then please follow the links below.

https://www.facebook.com/Nigel-Shinner-1394054230917164/?fref=ts

https://twitter.com/nigel_shinner

Made in the USA
Charleston, SC
13 November 2015